PRAISE FOR

"Thor, Baldacci, Flynn, Hamburg. Get ready as Banner fits right in!"

AMAZON REVIEW

"Move over Jack Reacher there's a new guy taking over."

AMAZON REVIEW

"Great stuff. Exciting and fast paced. On par with Flynn & Thor."

AMAZON REVIEW

"The writing was superior, the story line was compelling and the action was top-notch. Sorry I could only give this one a five star rating!"

AMAZON REVIEW

ROGUE KILL

A HARRY BAUER THRILLER

BLAKE BANNER

RIGHTHOUSE

The characters and events portrayed in this ebook are fictitious. Any similarity to real persons, living or dead, is coincidental and not intended by the author.

ISBN-13: 978-1-63696-184-2

ISBN-10: 1-63696-184-3

Cover design by: Damonza

Printed in the United States of America

www.righthouse.com

www.instagram.com/righthousebooks

www.facebook.com/righthousebooks

twitter.com/righthousebooks

HARRY BAUER THRILLER SERIES

Dead of Night (Book 1)
Dying Breath (Book 2)
The Einstaat Brief (Book 3)
Quantum Kill (Book 4)
Immortal Hate (Book 5)
The Silent Blade (Book 6)
LA: Wild Justice (Book 7)
Breath of Hell (Book 8)
Invisible Evil (Book 9)
The Shadow of Ukupacha (Book 10)
Sweet Razor Cut (Book 11)
Blood of the Innocent (Book 12)
Blood on Balthazar (Book 13)
Simple Kill (Book 14)
Riding The Devil (Book 15)
The Unavenged (Book 16)
The Devil's Vengeance (Book 17)
Bloody Retribution (Book 18)
Rogue Kill (Book 19)
Blood for Blood (Book 20)

ONE

My cell rang. I sat up and looked at the phone. It was Colonel Jane Harris, my ex head of operations. It was three in the morning. The glass in my windows was black. I put the phone to my ear.

"Jane. Is there a problem?"

"Yes." Her voice was quiet, like she didn't want to be heard. I wondered for a moment if she was drunk, but that wasn't her style.

"Where are you?"

"I need you to listen carefully and not interrupt."

"Shoot."

"I am staking out some men—"

"You're doing *what?*"

"I need your help, Harry. I haven't got time for bullshit. I am a CIA officer, remember? I think I may have been compromised, and I have nobody else to call on—"

I suppressed a rush of rage. I got as far as, "You have no one to —" and stopped. "Where are you?"

"You know the Bayonne area of New Jersey? Bergen Point? Constable Hook—"

"I know the area. Where?"

"Avenue F and East 24th Street. I'm in a dark Volkswagen Golf, right on the corner."

I had her on the bedside table and spoke as I pulled on my clothes.

"How many of them are there?"

"So far four. I don't know if they've called for backup."

"What makes you think you're compromised?"

"They're parked outside a mosque down the road. They were out of their vehicles talking, and after a while they started looking up the road. I was pretty sure they were looking at me. Then one of them made a call."

"Get out of there."

"I can't."

I shoved my Fairbairn and Sykes in my boot and pulled on my Sig Sauer P226 as I rasped, "Why the hell not? You could have eight guys there in the next two minutes. You'll be lucky if they just shoot you!" I was running down the stairs taking them three at a time. "It's going to take me half an hour minimum to get there!"

"I haven't got time to argue with you, Harry!"

"Why? What else are you doing? Watching four guys? You can't watch and talk at the same time? I need to know the facts, Jane!"

I was out the door and taking the stoop in two strides. My car was a damned TVR. Cerbera Speed Eight. It was going to stand out like a luminous dildo at a vicar's tea party. But I had no choice, and it would at least get me there fast. I slid behind the wheel and fired up the big four hundred and forty V8 engine while she told me, "These are very bad men, Harry." I floored the pedal and did zero to sixty in less than four seconds, leaving behind the stench of burned rubber. I hit Harlem River Drive closing on a hundred and didn't fishtail when I turned north.

The colonel was saying, "We have Russian Mafia here talking to Iranians, and we have identified at least four chemists among their contacts tonight. I need to know what's going down."

I snapped, "If you've been compromised, whatever they *had* going down won't go down until you are dead, or worse, abducted for interrogation."

I was doing one-twenty hurtling north beside the black river, making for the George Washington Bridge, feeling the few seconds we had trickling away.

"I know that. That's why I haven't called Buddy. He'll order me to abort. But I know, Harry, I *know* what's going down tonight is important. I *can't* walk away. It's why I called you."

"You *need* to call the brigadier!"

"*I can't!*" she hissed. "If they move in, they'll blow it!"

I thought about calling the brigadier myself. Though I had no priority access anymore, I still had his private number. But I wanted to stay connected with the colonel in case anything went down. I needed to hear everything that happened. Right on cue, she whispered, "*I have to go.*"

I hollered, "*No! Leave the call open!*" But I was shouting at a dead cell.

I crossed the George Washington Bridge like I was jet-propelled, yelling at Siri to call the brigadier. She took her time calling, and he took his time answering. My calls were no longer considered a possible emergency. I hurtled around Overpeck Park closing on a hundred and forty miles an hour with the brigadier saying to me, "Harry, this is not a good time—"

"With all due respect, sir, shut up and listen. The colonel called me ten or fifteen minutes ago. She believes she is compromised. She did not want to inform you in case you told her to abort. I am on my way. Estimated arrival five minutes. Avenue F and East 24th Street, Bayonne. She's in a dark Volkswagen Golf on the corner. She just hung up on me saying she had to go."

His reply was "Ten-four. Over," and he was gone.

I started braking as I approached the docks, and the tires complained as I turned right onto 30th Street. After that it was a fight against myself to keep the speed and the noise down. It took only a couple of seconds for me to realize that keeping a TVR quiet was never going to happen. Its looks and the sound it makes are going to get you noticed. So I found a channel that played the kind of thudding noise guys who wear shades at night like to snort coke to and turned the volume up so high my windshield started to vibrate. Then I covered the six hundred yards to East 24th in twenty seconds and turned the corner real slow. There was no sign of a Golf anywhere. I pulled up by the grass shoulder like I was stoned or drunk and sat and had a look around. I could feel my heart pounding hard high up in my chest. I ignored it and forced myself to focus on every minute detail.

There was junk and trash all around me. Open land fenced off on my right, on my left a large, windowless building, then a couple of houses and at the end, wasteland and, hidden from view by trees and a couple of cars, a building my GPS said was a mosque.

It was from that hidden area that a man now walked out. His shadow was cast long across the road by the limpid orange light from the building. He was tall, big-shouldered, in jeans and a leather jacket. He stopped in the middle of the road and stared toward me. I knew all he could see was my headlights, and all he could hear was the thudding of my music.

He looked back the way he'd come, like he was talking. Another guy, just as tall but slimmer, joined him. He didn't take long to think it through. He started walking up the road with his big pal just behind him.

Whichever way you looked at it, there was no plus side to the situation. I made a note in the back of my mind always to have a suppressed twenty-two semi in the car. But all I had right then was a 9 mm Sig and a knife sharp enough to split atoms. I toyed with the idea of plowing into them. If I let them get close enough, I could hit them at forty miles per hour in less than two seconds. But I'd be damned if I let these sons of bitches dent a twenty-year-old TVR Cerbera Speed Eight.

When they were pulling level with the hood, I made a show of trying to climb out and stumbling to the ground, clinging to the door like I had no control over my limbs. I stayed like that, on all fours, for a couple of seconds until I heard the tall, lean guy's footsteps reaching me. Then I got on one foot and one knee and grinned a stupid, drooling grin at him. His face said he didn't know whether to kick me, shoot me, or just bundle me back into my car. His pal was closing in behind him. He said something in Persian as I got to my feet and swayed dangerously. I said, "You are a *pal*" as I laughed and lurched forward.

I reached for his shoulder with my left hand, and his instinctive reaction was to grip my arm with his right. The movement of the knife was so fast he didn't even know he'd been stabbed. It went through his esophagus, his windpipe, and his spinal nerve in a quarter of a second. His friend saw him stumble and attributed it to the drunken asshole who'd just fallen against him. By the time he'd realized he was wrong, his friend had fallen to his knees with blood gushing from this throat, and it was too late. It was too late because I had stumbled past the dying man and rammed the Fairbairn and Sykes through his right eye, making a real mess of his brain.

He went down quietly. It's hard to make a noise when your speech center is all mixed up with your autonomic digestive center and your optic nerve.

I hesitated for just a moment. The thing would have been to take the Cerbera down to the mosque and get the colonel out of there fast. But making a quiet approach with a TVR Cerbera is like trying to make a silent approach with ten Harley Davidsons. So I killed the radio and the engine and sprinted down to the corner of the building from which the two guys had emerged.

The mosque was a dilapidated two-story building. At some point in the past, somebody had painted it white. Since then, it had turned an unhealthy shade of gray turned slightly yellow by two distant street lamps. I pressed up against the wall, hunkered down into the shadows, and peered around into a yard behind a wire mesh fence with a big gate in it. The gate was open and big enough for a truck to fit through. The yard was maybe thirty or forty feet long and twenty feet across, with two garages at the far end. One of those had the roller blind up, and inside I could see a dark Golf.

There was a murmur of voices, one, maybe two low and male, one female, quiet but sounding very much like the colonel when she was mad.

I slipped through the gate and took a tangent track to the door of the open garage. There I stopped and took a moment to listen. There was a guy talking. He had a deep voice and an accent. It wasn't Russian.

"We can call police," he was saying. "I need know why you are here, alone in your car, this time of night, outside our mosque."

The colonel's voice came clear and crisp. "Please do! Call the police! This is effectively kidnapping! How dare you force me in here—"

"Shut up, woman." He said it without any real feeling. "Why you are here? You are whore waiting for client? But you don't look like whore. So what? You are spy?"

"You have asked me the same, insulting, offensive question fifty times already! And I have told you that I am an American citizen and I have a perfect right to be on any American public road I please without having to give *you* an explanation! Now will you *please* give me back the keys to my—"

"I can make you talk."

I had heard enough, and the heavy silence that followed his words told me it was time to do something. I wondered for a fraction of a second how long the brigadier was going to take to get there, then I stepped into the garage, smiling.

I had expected two guys and the colonel. What I saw surprised me, and if I had known, I would have taken a different approach. But it was too late. I was committed.

Colonel Jane Harris was sitting on a low stool with her back to a work bench. Standing in front of her, leaning his back against her Volkswagen was a big guy with a big belly and a big, black beard. In that moment he was staring at me with something between contempt and indifference.

Beyond him, leaning against the far wall, were three more guys. Two of them were holding AK 12 assault rifles. The third was holding a long screwdriver, turning it over in his fingers. I noted absently that to the left of the hood there was a closed door.

I said, "It was just some drunk guy in a foreign car who had the radio on. They're giving him a good kicking right now."

By the time I'd finished, they were all frowning. The big guy said, "Who are you?"

I gave a small laugh and said, "Right?" Simultaneously, I shot the two guys with the AK12s. The guy with the screwdriver leaped and rolled behind the car, and I smashed my foot into the side of the big guy's knee. He screamed, and I yelled at Jane, "*Get your key!*"

She was on it, and I went around her car looking for the guy with the screwdriver. I found him on all fours scrabbling at the door. He was quick. I fired, but he had the door open and rolled through. I was going after him, but I could see the colonel across the roof. Her face was twisted with rage, looking down at the floor, where she appeared to be kicking the big guy.

I snapped, "Have you got the key?"

"*Yes!*" She snarled it through her teeth with one last kick.

"*Get in!*"

She wrenched open the door and clambered in. I got behind the wheel. We slammed the doors, fired up the engine, and reversed out at speed. I spun the wheel as we went ass-first out the gate and made the tires squeal as we surged up the road toward the Cerbera.

"Get ready to jump and run for the TVR!" I yanked up the handbrake and twisted the wheel so we spun on a dime and screeched to a halt, with me on the driver's side of the Cerbera and the colonel on the passenger side. I bellowed, "*Now!*" and we shoved open the doors and ran for the TVR beast.

As we did so, I heard the rattle of automatic fire behind us.

Jane yanked open the passenger door and slipped in. As I pulled open my door, I saw the Golf shudder and the windows shatter.

I got behind the wheel, made the big V8 growl, and reversed my ass into Avenue F. I slammed in first and made zero to sixty in three and a half seconds. I jumped the lights onto 440, and then we were hurtling toward I-95 and the George Washington Bridge.

I snarled at my cell, "Siri, call the brigadier!"

It rang once, then, "We're on our way. Where are you?"

"In my Cerbera headed north on I-95 toward the George Washington Bridge."

"You have Jane?"

"The colonel is with me. There are four men dead at the mosque on East 24th, one badly beaten and one armed who shot at us as we left. They have Russian AK 12s."

"You are both uninjured?"

"Yeah—"

I looked at the colonel. Her eyes were glazed, her mouth was sagging, and her skin looked yellow. I felt the acid burn of fear in my belly, but my voice was ice-cold when I said, "Correction. The colonel is hit." I reached over and felt her wrist for a pulse. I said, "Critical. Barely a pulse. We're losing her."

His voice was equally cold when he said, "I'll meet you at Teterboro with a chopper. We're on our way."

He hung up, and I floored the pedal. The Cerbera will do a hundred and ninety-five miles per hour. I think we got close on the way to the airport.

TWO

We stood on the tarmac and watched the chopper rise into the predawn blackness. The last thing the doctor had said to the brigadier before he climbed in beside his patient was, "Prepare yourself, Buddy. She might go tonight. She's unlikely to make it."

The brigadier had nodded, like he'd been told his groceries were going to arrive fifteen minutes late. Then he turned, and we'd walked in silence back to my car.

Once there, I asked him, "Where are you taking her?"

"We have cutting-edge facilities at Pleasantville."

"Who was she investigating?"

"You know I can't tell you that, Harry. You resigned."

"You need a ride?"

He nodded. "Yes, thank you."

I didn't ask him where he wanted to go, and he didn't tell me. We just climbed in the car, I pulled out of the airport, and we headed for Manhattan. We covered the distance in silence, crossed from Fort Lee to Fort Washington, came off onto Riverside Drive, and slowly ambled down to Broadway as far as 133rd before turning west and weaving my way home, all in absolute silence.

Finally I pulled up outside my brownstone and killed the

engine. The sky was turning pale, and the streetlamps were burning against a clear sky. I said, like I was talking to the steering wheel, "I didn't ask, but I figured you could use a drink. You want breakfast?"

Now I looked at him, and he nodded. "Yes, breakfast and a shot would be good. Thank you."

I let him in and closed the door, and he followed me into the kitchen, where he sat at the big pine table while I scrambled eggs, made coffee, and poured us each a stiff shot of Bushmills.

I finished the eggs and toast and placed his plate in front of him. He nodded, and I noticed he hadn't touched his whiskey or his coffee. I raised my glass.

"Cheers!"

His eyes searched my face for a couple of seconds before he replied.

"Yes, cheers!"

He knocked it back, set down his glass, and picked up his fork.

"Harry, you left Cobra. I can't tell you anything about what Jane was doing."

I frowned as I chewed. I swallowed, drained my cup, and refilled it.

"Sir, everything Cobra does is completely illegal. We—you—murder people routinely in breach of the laws of every democracy in the Western world, but you are concerned about breaking Cobra's own rules on confidentiality? Rules that don't even have the status of laws?"

He sighed and forced himself to eat some of the egg.

"It may seem absurd to you, Harry—"

"There is no 'may' about it, sir. Forgive me for being blunt, but it's stupid. It is the exact antithesis of what you drilled into us every day. Prepare and train as much as is humanly possible, but once you are in the field, be prepared to adapt and improvise at a moment's notice."

He stared at me a moment and said, "Adapt and improvise" with no particular intonation.

"You always told us the objective was to win, and to win, we must use every resource available to us."

"Yes," he said and stuffed egg in his mouth. "Every available resource."

"I am an available resource, sir. You know I am good, and you know you can trust me. Use me."

"You chose to resign. Why this now?"

"You know the answer to that as well as I do. This is the colonel..." I trailed off, searching for words that would both convey the pain and the fear we were both feeling but at the same time hide those very things. In the end, I said, "We owe it to her."

"Yes," he said and picked up his cup.

"We are from the Regiment, sir. We are blades. We do things differently. Our way."

"All right, Harry. We are going to have a conversation that never happened. It never happened because after breakfast I called for my car and left."

"That's what happened."

"So it would have been impossible for us to have this conversation."

"What conversation?"

He smiled in a way that spoke more of weariness than humor. "Have you heard of a man called Nick Galkin?"

I shook my head. "No, never."

He nodded in an abstracted way, looking at the kitchen floor. "He keeps a pretty low profile. His father was Russian. He claimed to have worked for the KGB, but when the Soviet Union collapsed, he moved into the private sector, where he became a modest billionaire, moved to the United States, and married an American woman of breeding. Daddy is the kind of man who makes and unmakes presidents. So young Nick was already a very powerful man before he was even born, in 1990."

"That makes him 34."

"And a billionaire in his own right."

"How does he make his money?"

"That is a good question, and one we and the CIA spent many, many man-hours on. In brief, it goes something like this: Nick has created a number of shell companies on off-shore fiscal havens. In practically all of these cases, the companies are owned by other companies which are in turn owned by corporations. So they are hard to track down."

"Okay. What does he do with these companies?"

"In essence, what he does is identify countries that have trade embargos against them. Let's say, for example, that sanctions against a Middle Eastern country mean it can't sell oil to some of its usual trading partners—say France and Germany, the European Union. But the tiny Pacific Island of King George has no such embargo against—let's call it Iraqistan. So Nick has a trading company registered in King George, and he buys from Iraqistan a couple of oil tankers' worth of crude oil."

"He still can't sell it to Europe because the provenance is Iraqistan."

"Correct, but what he can do is sell it to the White Russian Trading Corporation, which is registered on the island of Bintan in Indonesia. From there, the cargo is transferred to another ship, where the bill of lading shows the petroleum as being bought and sold in Indonesia, and from there, through perhaps another couple of buyers and sellers, all belonging to our Nick, the goods arrive after a short delay, though at a considerably higher price, in Europe."

We sat in silence for a while. Then I said, "If the product you're dealing with is oil, you can almost write it off as a resourceful man surviving in the dog-eat-dog world of international commerce." The brigadier nodded. I said, "But something tells me we are not just talking about oil."

"That something would be dead right. With the help of his father, he has spent some twenty years building up a network of shell companies and holding corporations that defy Western jurisdiction. He can pretty much move anything anywhere he wants. And he has made three very big, very powerful friends—"

"China, Russia, and Iran."

"Intelligence from all the Five Eyes and Israel suggests very strongly that he is moving not just chemicals for chemical weapons but essential components for nuclear bombs. But nobody can prove it. The CIA approached us through Jane and asked us to take care of him but also to try and get some access to his network—either to close him down or destroy it. It's not a needle in a haystack, quite the opposite. It's more like a three-dimensional spiderweb enmeshed in a haystack."

"And that's what Jane was doing?"

He looked at me for a long time. He looked gray and drawn.

"That's her job, Harry. She's a highly capable CIA officer. She would not thank me for treating her like an incompetent girl."

"I know that."

He frowned. "I don't understand quite why she called you, and it was you who called me..." He shook his head. "Why didn't she call me directly for backup?"

I gave a smile you could call rueful. "I asked her the same question while I was falling down the stairs pulling my clothes on. She said she was worried you'd abort the mission."

"She was right. And I think the outcome shows it would have been the right decision." He reached across the table and gripped my wrist. "That is no reflection on you, Harry. What you did was extraordinary in itself. Nobody could have guarded against what was ultimately a lucky shot. Or an unlucky one, depending on who you are..." He trailed off.

I nodded. "What's that old Viking thing? Fearlessness is better than a faint heart for any man who would poke his nose out of doors. The length of my life and the day of my death were fated long ago."

"By the Norn, indeed. Let us stay positive and believe firmly that that day has not come yet for Jane."

We drank to that, and I distributed more whiskey.

"So brass tacks, sir."

He gave his head a twitch. "It's not quite that easy. The way I see it, the mission comes in two parts. The first part is well within your capability."

"Kill him and his immediate ring."

"Yes, but the second part is more complicated. Close down his network."

"I can do that."

He frowned at me. "How, for God's sake?"

"I need to talk to your smartest IT nerd. We need to put together a virus that combines the worst elements of the worst viruses to date." I counted some off on my fingers. "Stuxnet, Cryptolocker, Zeus, Mydoom."

"For what purpose, precisely?"

"To identify his companies using artificial intelligence and spread through them, shutting them down as it goes. Any funds found in their accounts are diverted to Cobra, and I trust you to give me fifty percent as spoils of war."

"That's fair enough, but there is the small matter of the delivery system. How on earth do you plan to deliver this mega-virus?"

"That's the simplest part of all, sir. He will introduce it into his system himself, only he will think it is money he is receiving. But the figure will be a code for the virus to ride in piggyback and invisible."

He was quiet for a long time. Finally he said, "That is actually a very good idea. You would pose as a client, representing a major commercial interest. You buy the product and pay. The virus rides in on the money."

He stabbed at his scrambled eggs with his fork for a while, then drank his coffee and finished his Bushmills. Finally he set down his glass and sighed.

"Harry. This could work. I am going to talk to our IT department. They may want to have a discreet word with you. Meanwhile I'll have a copy of the colonel's file sent over. We are not employing you, so you shall have to decide yourself who goes down and who is allowed to live."

I shrugged and made a face. "In my experience, people tend to do that themselves."

He nodded. "Your body count was talked about at the mess in the Regiment, and now it is discussed at Cobra. No complaints from me." He stood. "I'll be in touch later today."

He called for his car, and ten minutes later, I watched him walk to the Bentley, climb in, and drive away. He had offered me a number I could call to stay up to date with the colonel's progress, but I declined. I figured as long as nobody called me, that would be good news.

I told him, "Let me know when she's out of surgery. The rest we'll take a day at a time."

I closed the door on the morning and lay on the sofa in the bay window turning things over in my mind. Getting close to Nick Galkin was not going to be easy, and I wondered if the colonel had developed any kind of plan herself. The answer came twenty minutes later when a biker rang the bell and handed me a sealed parcel.

When I opened it, it contained evidence of what I had always known: that the colonel was thorough to the point of being fastidious and highly organized.

Much of her research I had already been through with the brigadier. In addition to that, there were photographs of a large number of men, including the four I had killed that night, the one she had seriously maimed or killed herself, and the one who had ultimately shot her. These, and a number of others, were listed as Iranian intelligence staff attached to the Iranian Permanent Mission to the United Nations.

She had intelligence from the CIA that Nick Galkin was in New York and had attended several meetings both at the UN and at private apartments. His meetings made interesting reading.

He had visited Arav Yasdi, the secretary to the ambassador on several occasions, both at the UN Building and at Third Avenue.

What was more interesting was his three meetings with Xie Ken, the Chinese Ambassador to the United Nations. One of those had been at the UN, and the other two had been at the Plaza Hotel. Those meetings constituted what President Bush in his day would have called the Axis of Evil: a Russian ex-KGB officer meeting with high-ranking Iranian and Chinese diplomats in private. It was interesting but not surprising.

What was surprising was his series of meetings with Stavros Moustakas, the European Union's Ambassador to the United Nations, not to mention the private meetings at the private apartments of Adam Schmidt, the first secretary to the secretary for defense of the German Federal Republic. That was on the Monday. On the Wednesday, he'd dined with M Julia Garnier, the personal secretary to the Minister of the Armed Forces of France. And Friday, he had dined at the palatial home of Oscar Hansen on 69th Street. Hansen was the famous, infamous, and notorious Danish arms dealer, notable among other things for helping to establish the largest Buddhist temple in Europe. At that same dinner, there had been CEOs and heads of department from the McDaniels Skyline Rat Labs, Anglo-American Petrochemicals, Global Chemicals of Texas, and Nevada Delivery Systems, to name but a few.

I spoke aloud, absently, like the colonel was sitting in the chair across from me.

"So if we assume, just for a moment, that the Axis of Evil—Iran, Russia, and China—are Nick Galkin's clients, and we take a look at the other people he has been talking to, what do we find they have in common?"

The words hung in the air because there was nobody to answer them. I raised my thumb. "The French and the German were attached to their respective ministries of defense; the Dane is an arms dealer. Then, the notable guests at the major function that week and the Danish arms dealer's house were McDaniels Skyline Rat Labs, Anglo-American Petrochemicals, Global Chemicals of Texas, and Nevada Delivery Systems, all defense contractors, all at the cutting edge of military technology, and all part of what Dwight Eisenhower had termed the Military-Industrial Complex.

"So what does that mean?" I asked the air. "That American defense contractors are selling cutting-edge military technology to our enemies?"

I read on. The colonel had believed to begin with that Iran was trying to build a dirty bomb or some kind of biological or chemical weapon that it could deploy against Israel. But the more research she had done and the further she had investigated, the clearer it had become that this went well beyond a single weapon.

I paused and closed my eyes. My memory was reaching for something a Dutch Admiral in NATO had said recently. The guy had the same name as me: Bauer. And he had said that the civilian population should prepare, because war with Russia had become inevitable.

THREE

"NOT EVERYTHING IS GOING TO BE HUNKY-DORY IN THE next 20 years." He'd been talking about the the Steadfast Defender Exercise which was taking place across Europe at the time. It had more than doubled in size since it was announced in 2023 and was explicitly designed to prepare the alliance for a Russian invasion. But NATO officials had been anxious because both Western governments and private sector arms manufacturers were slacking, scaling down armies and production, reducing their capability to respond in a crisis. Yet while Western military budgets were dwindling and stockpiles of weapons and ammunition had been drained by the conflict in Ukraine and would take years to replenish, Russia had tripled its military expenditure to forty percent of the entire national budget.

I closed my eyes again and recalled his face with clear, anxious, intelligent eyes.

"We need to have a system in place to find more people if it comes to war. And we need to be able to fall back on an industrial base that is able to produce weapons and ammunition fast enough to be able to continue a conflict if we get into one."

And Boris Pistorious, the German defense minister, had said the West could face all-out war with Russia in five to eight years.

the growing dark, first of suburbia and then the semi-countryside of Yonkers and Elmsford. After half an hour, I came to the winding lanes and woodlands of Pleasantville, where I followed the searching, yellow funnels of my headlights out of town and along Bedford Road, where trees and mailboxes sprang out of shadowy lawns, throwing black shadows back across their front yards like spindly, inky demons. Until finally I found Apple Hill Lane and the big iron gates of Cobra HQ.

The latest in voice recognition and iris scanning technology told security I was probably Harry Bauer, and if I wasn't I was using some badass artificial intelligence that would probably bring about the end of civilization as we knew it. Fortunately, the first option was right, the gate swung open, and ten minutes later, I was stepping across the checkerboard floor of the entrance hall toward the brigadier's study-cum-library. Through the heavy walnut door, I found the brigadier seated at the large fireplace with three other men. They all turned to look at me as he got to his feet.

"Harry, good of you to join us. These gentlemen are: Army General John Moorcroft, of the Joint Chiefs of Staff, General Schwarz of the Marines and personal advisor to the President, and Admiral Sam Benner, also advisor to the president. Gentlemen, this is Harry Bauer, of whom I have spoken to you at some length."

The admiral cocked a rueful smile and said, "I'm reminded of that song, 'You Picked a Fine Time to Leave Me, Lucille.' If half of what Buddy tells us is true, you are the man we need right now, Harry."

I nodded my appreciation, and the brigadier waved me to a chair. I sat while he poured me a Bushmills.

General Moorcroft of the Joint Chiefs of Staff cleared his throat. "I am stating the obvious," he said. "But sometimes the obvious has to be stated, and then it usually falls to men like me to state it." They all chuckled amiably, nodding, suggesting they had all been called on from time to time to state the obvious. It was a select club, and they all belonged to it. "This meeting is not happening, and none of us is here."

The brigadier tried not to sigh and failed. "Yes, John, I am sure we are all clear on that. Both murder and assassination are still against the law in this country, even for four-star generals. And that is what we are here to plan and ultimately execute."

Schwartz gave his head a small twitch. "You talk as straight as you shoot, Buddy. The way I like it. No wasting time.

"Gentlemen, we are facing the possibility—indeed the *probability*—of all-out war with the united forces of Iran, Russia, and China armed with chemical and biological weapons of mass destruction with which we are completely unfamiliar. All the intelligence we have suggests that these weapons are novel, innovative, and lethal in the extreme."

Admiral Benner sighed and addressed his very shiny shoes, which were crossed at his ankles in front of the fire.

"We have been here before, Buddy. Weapons of mass destruction..." He trailed off, like the words spoke for themselves.

The brigadier arched an eyebrow at him, and the temperature of the room seemed to drop ten degrees.

"This is not intelligence gathered from the Internet, Sam, or sourced from brown-nosed president pleasers. We are talking about intelligence gathered by actual professionals, by us for us. And I can assure you our purposes were not political, but military."

The admiral was unfazed but didn't answer. He just sipped his whiskey. The brigadier went on.

"The West's response to Ukraine and Gaza has been exactly what Putin and the ayatollahs had hoped for and expected. Seventy years after World War Two, Western politicians have no stomach for global war."

. . .

General Schwarz snorted. "They have no stomach, period. For global war, regional war, or facing down a bunch of kids with pierced noses and woolen hats! And it's not the only damned organ they're missing!"

There was some muttering of agreement from the admiral and General Moorcroft. The brigadier suppressed a smile and continued.

"With the help of Nick Galkin and his extensive global network, it looks as though the three powers, Russia, China, and Iran have been able to put together some kind of biological or chemical weapon." He paused, nodding. "If—*if*—we are lucky, it is a weapon and not an arsenal which they have put together. Otherwise we are facing an *existential* threat, gentlemen. And I do not mean that figuratively. I mean it literally: our very existence as a society, as a culture, is in imminent threat of annihilation."

He paused again, looking at each of them in turn. Then he concluded,

"And we face this existential threat without a captain at the helm, without a leader who has the stomach, the backbone"—he smiled at Schwartz—"or the balls to take the necessary action to stop the enemy. There is nothing to be gained by moaning or griping about that. The question we face here tonight is: in the confronted with this threat, what action are *we* going to take?"

General John Moorcroft of the Joint Chiefs of Staff gave a big bark of a laugh. "Why do I get the feeling, Buddy, that this is a question you have asked and answered already?"

The brigadier ignored the question, except that he looked at Moorcroft for a moment. Then he addressed them all.

"I have a proposal for you. You can take it or leave it, but if you leave it, you had better have a damned good alternative. I will outline it in broad strokes for you, and later, if you want to, we can go into the finer details—though the less you know, the better. In broad terms, it is this: We deploy Harry Bauer to assassinate Nick Galkin at the earliest possible opportunity, no later than the next two or three days. Galkin will not be his sole target.

He will also eliminate Galkin's personal assistant of the last five years, Anniken Larsen, who is widely tipped to become his heir and successor.

"Secondary targets once Galkin and Larsen are taken care of need to be discussed but could potentially include: Stavros Moustakas, the European Union's Ambassador to the United Nations, Adam Schmidt, the first secretary to the secretary for Defense of the German Federal Republic, M Julia Garnier, the personal secretary to the Minister of the Armed Forces of France, and Oscar Hansen, a Danish arms dealer. We have also a B list of CEOs and heads of department from the McDaniels Skyline's Rat Labs, Anglo-American Petrochemicals, Global Chemicals of Texas, and Nevada Delivery Systems."

General John Moorcroft was scowling hard. "You better slow down there, Buddy. You planning on leaving anyone alive?"

I leaned forward and addressed the brigadier. "May I answer this, sir?"

He looked mildly surprised, which wasn't something he did often. He said, "By all means, Harry."

I turned to Moorcroft. "General, I have lost count of the number of men I have killed, both in combat on special operations and since I have been an associate of the brigadier. I have an exceptional record of kills. I wouldn't be at this meeting if that were not the case. But the reason for my kill rate—and my survival rate—is not down to exceptional combat skills. It is in great part due to understanding a very important principle. And that principle is that when you are fighting, whether it be a fist fight or a global nuclear conflict, you are communicating with your opponent."

They all frowned at me at the same time. I ignored them and went on.

"I learned this as a kid on the streets in the Bronx. I was twelve years old, and Benito Gomez and four of his pals stopped me on the way home and tried to take my money and my new shades. I crippled Benito, and I'm pretty sure he never had any kids when he grew up. I could have left it at that. I could have walked away."

I sipped my whiskey, and as I set down the glass, I said, "But I realized even back then that I was not just fighting. I was communicating. What had I told them? I am mean in a fight, but if enough of you come for me, you'll win. That wasn't enough. So as soon as Benito was down, I went after his cousin and blinded him in one eye with a finger jab. While he was screaming, I stabbed the biggest of the remaining two in the gut and broke his knee. The fourth guy tried to get away, but I caught him and broke all his fingers." I paused a moment, nodding slowly. "Now I had communicated that if they came after me, there would be a very high price to pay. It would *not* be proportionate. That is the message we need to send to the Kremlin, Beijing, and Tehran. The come-back for them, and for anyone who wants to join them, will be well beyond proportionate. Otherwise they will just keep coming."

They were quiet for a while until Admiral Benner said, "You really did that?"

"Yes, sir. Every time I have felt threatened, I communicate to my opponent that it will not be worth his will. The price will be too high."

Schwartz grinned suddenly and chuckled. "I see why you like this guy, Buddy." To me, he said, "We could use a few more like him in Congress, God dammit!"

He drained his glass and pointed at the brigadier. "I'll tell you what I am going to do. I am going to take these two pansies to Keens Steakhouse for dinner. Because there is nothing left to discuss here. I trust your judgment, and I especially trust *his* judgment!" He stabbed a finger in my direction. "Do what you gotta do and count on our support as far as we can legally provide it. And as far as I am concerned, you can take out as many of those bastards as you think you need to." He stood. "C'mon, boys. Those steaks ain't gonna eat themselves!"

We all stood, and the brigadier saw them out. A couple of minutes later, he returned and closed the door.

"I'll order some sandwiches," he said. "Then we'll work through the night. We'll prepare a kill list and a precise plan." He gave his head a small shake. "You can't take care of all of them, but I'll give you the principal ones and have other operatives hit the secondary targets. I assume you are onboard."

"I'm onboard," I said, "and I am ready to communicate."

FOUR

He bit into a whole-wheat sandwich of roast beef and horseradish sauce and spoke with his mouth full.

"Galkin does not have an apartment in New York. Rumor has it he once tried to buy an apartment on West 59th—well, strictly Central Park South—and he was blackballed. Since then he has hated New York." He swallowed and bit again. "He's one of those Russians who claims to hate all things American but tries extraordinarily hard to *be* American. You get it a lot with the French too," he added absently. "Always mouthing off about *les Américains ignorants,* but they listen to jazz, watch American films, and eat at McDonalds."

I raised an eyebrow as he devoured the rest of his sandwich and reached for his whiskey.

"Did you forget to eat today?"

"Yes. So Nick Galkin is staying at the Aman on 5th Avenue at the Grand Suite. I'll book you into the Corner Suite. He seems to be here for several meetings with an eclectic group of people, but we know there is also a week-long conference at the hotel: 'Shipping in the 21st Century.'"

"Could be more interesting than it sounds." He glanced at me like he thought I was trying to be funny. I shrugged. "Pirates, sailing across the poles, ships powered by sail wings..."

"Yes," he said and reached for another sandwich. "Precisely. He will be at the conference. We'll book you in there too. It may be the only opportunity you have to approach him. From what we have been able to observe, most of the time, he is surrounded by pretty tight security. One advantage you'll have, of course, is that he has tended to keep a very low profile."

I reached for a sandwich. "Why is that an advantage?"

He chewed and swallowed. "Because it will be perfectly credible that you don't know he is a shipping magnate. You just happen to get into conversation and mention you are looking to buy some merchandise for your principal, but you need to do some creative shipping."

I nodded. "Okay."

"You need to get the negotiations over and done with as soon as possible. You tell him your principal has a very short window." He nodded a few times while he chewed, as though he were agreeing with some internal dialogue. "It is, of course, we who have a short window. We need to get the sale made, his execution and the execution of his close associates carried out almost simultaneously, and within the next few days."

I sipped my whiskey and thought for a moment. Then, "Have we got the virus?"

"I'll know later tonight."

"Okay. There is one more thing I need."

"Name it."

"A phone call."

He frowned at me, and I explained what I wanted. He thought about it for a while. I knew it was a tall order, but as far as I could see, it was the only way to be sure of pulling off the sting. In the end, he called his director of IT and the director of AI and had them come up to talk to us.

Apparently they were called Thumb and Dark Avenger, or Dark for short. Thumb was about two hundred and ninety pounds of pure genius in dirty jeans and a black AC/DC T-shirt with lank black hair that hadn't been washed since last century. His pal, Dark, was six-three and seemed to be composed of bone with a layer of stretched skin over the top. He was bald on top but managed to eek out a braid that reached his ass. His T-shirt said that Gillian Anderson refused to return his shorts.

We talked for about an hour, and I sat and sipped whiskey and watched two nerds in their late forties getting virtually excited. Pretty soon, they had forgotten the brigadier and I were there and had withdrawn into their own two-dimensional world where they argued passionately about back doors, Trojans, worms, and dragons.

At two a.m., the brigadier asked them, "Gentlemen, can you do it or not?"

The one with the unwashed hair and the AC/DC T-shirt said, "Yes!"

The bald one with the braid said, "No."

"Give me an answer by breakfast. Make it a yes."

They left, grumbling, and returned to the basement where they lived. When the door had closed, the brigadier took a deep breath.

"Leave your TVR here. Take the Bentley. We'll discuss your back story over breakfast."

We sat in silence for a while. Eventually I said, "Any news?"

"Nothing yet. You'll be the first to know, Harry, as soon as they call me."

"Thanks."

I climbed the stairs to the room I had always used before. It was still laid out as I had had it. That depressed me, for some reason. I showered and brushed my teeth and lay and watched the small hours turn into dawn. Finally I managed to sleep from six till eight and rose to have breakfast with the brigadier.

Over eggs, bacon, and pancakes, he told me the colonel was out of surgery but in intensive care, and that Thumb and the Dark Avenger had agreed it could be done, but only because the

Avenger had managed to find a concealed path past the dragon Thumb hadn't even realized was there. Or perhaps it was the other way around. Either way, they could do it.

So at half past nine, I had taken the Bentley and driven back to Manhattan to pack a luxurious wardrobe and move into my Corner Suite at the Aman. As I'd moved silently through the suburban landscapes, I'd thought about everything I had discussed with the brigadier. He'd told me before I left that he was drawing up a secondary hit list of a few select CEOs and heads of department among the government's defense contractors—Ike's infamous military industrial complex—but these hits would go to other capable men and women.

He wanted me to focus on Nick Galkin and Anniken Larsen. Meanwhile, he would be drawing up plans for Stavros Moustakas, the European Union's Ambassador to the United Nations, Adam Schmidt, the first secretary to the secretary for Defense of the German Federal Republic, and M Julia Garnier, the personal secretary to the Minister of the Armed Forces of France.

I had asked him about Oscar Hansen, the Danish arms dealer, and he had made a strange face.

"The jury is still out on Oscar," he'd said. "But those three have to go."

It was a twenty-minute drive from my brownstone on James Baldwin Place to West 57th, if you enjoyed being crammed in with a million other people in the oppressive concrete environment of the FDR. But if you preferred driving your Bentley down 5th Avenue, enjoying the view of Central Park on a mid-morning in late spring, when women seem to acquire a particular glow, then it would take you some five or ten minutes longer. But to me, they were minutes well spent.

I tossed my keys to the valet, had two bellhops take my luggage from the trunk, and strolled into the foyer. The Aman is too cool and too elegant to have big cardboard cutouts of speakers indicating where your conference is taking place, but there was a discreet sign near the reception desk that said *THE FUTURE OF*

SHIPPING—RIDING THE WAVE. There was an arrow pointing toward the back of the foyer and beside it a stand with leaflets detailing the speakers and at what times they would be giving their talks.

I took a leaflet, checked in, and followed the bellhop up to my suite. I watched him open the curtains, show me the en suite bathroom, the living room, and all the unique rest of it and wondered what this kid would do for a few bucks. Bellhops had been useful to me in the past, and this guy was old enough to know the value of cash but young enough not to know the risks of gossip.

"I bet you get some interesting characters in this place, huh?"

"Yes, sir!"

"I'm a writer," I told him. "I write espionage thrillers. And you know an interesting thing?"

He could smell a big tip coming and planted a receptive smile on his face. I shoved my hands in my pockets and went and stared down at the traffic crawling past below with humans swarming on either side like ants.

"You might not believe it, kid, but most espionage these days is not done by governments." I turned to look at him. "It's done by industry, big multinational corporations. Industries, some of which are powerful enough to hold countries for ransom."

He nodded and twitched his head to on side. "I can believe that, sir."

"Yeah? You see things? Hear things?"

"Well, sir, not everybody is like you. You see a kid like me and you see a person. Most of the people who are rich enough to stay here see a bellhop uniform, like we are not really people, and they will talk incredibly freely about things you wouldn't believe possible."

"No kidding."

"Just the other day I was in the elevator and there were two guys talking about how he'd been in bed with the boss's girlfriend and he had to leave her because the boss called him to go 'deal with'"—he made inverted commas with his fingers—"a client who was refusing to cooperate."

"Man."

"Right?"

A good listener with absolutely no discretion.

"You want to make some extra cash?"

"I never say no to extra cash, sir."

"Good to know. But we have some ground rules. A, I pay you a hundred bucks for a complete snippet of useful information."

"Okay."

"B, you tell no one you are informing me. If you do, the very best that can happen to you is that you spend the next twenty years in jail."

He swallowed and said, "Okay" with a little less conviction.

"When I am gone, you forget completely that I was ever here. For reasons why, see B above, only it's worse. What's your name?"

"Sammy, sir. Sammy Glick."

"Sammy, I am not a writer."

"I know that, sir." He gave a small shrug. "The only writers who can afford this place are mega famous, and I have never seen or heard of you before."

"Good."

I reached in my jacket, allowing him to see the butt of my P226 and extracted a leather card holder in which I had placed a card I had made at home that said I was with the Department of Intelligence. I always carried it with me on gigs like this because it could often be useful.

"You have a guest here called Nick Galkin."

He nodded like a nod wasn't enough and he had to give it an extra something. "Yes, sir!"

I frowned. "Yeah?"

"Oh, yeah! He's the boss."

"The boss?"

"The *boss* the guy was talking about in the elevator!"

My eyebrows did a bit of climbing. “So you got the impression Mr. Galkin was a gangster?”

He gave a slightly lopsided smile. “Well, we were all pretty sure of that, sir, but not because of the conversation in the elevator. He has real tight security. We have pretty tight security, the electronics are cutting edge, as you can imagine. But he adds a whole nother layer on top.”

“Electronic?”

“No, sir. Nothing you could trace. Just plenty of big guys who don’t mind getting their hands dirty. You stray into one of the Galkin suites and next time anybody sees you, I figure you’ll be part of the foundations of a New Jersey shopping mall.”

"That’s funny.”

“In the Galkin suites, all the cameras are pointing *out*. They don’t want any video record of what happens inside.”

“Right.”

He grinned. “That’s how come the guard was sleeping with the girlfriend. No video.”

I pulled two hundred bucks from my wallet and held them up. “Make it three if you can tell me how many suites he has, where they are, who’s in them, and how many boys he’s got on special security.”

His smile turned vacant, and his eyes kind of glazed. “That is a lot of information, sir. And Mr. Galkin is a very dangerous man.”

“Four, and it had better be good.”

“Two suites on the next floor down. Turn right out of the elevator and it’s the last two doors. He’s in the apartment facing you, his girlfriend is in the room on the left, making a right angle. She won’t share with him, but he has another guy, his secretary or something, staying in his suite. Two gorillas with her, two with him, and four who come and go with his cars every day.”

I handed him the money. “If I die, Western Democracy will come looking for you.”

He took the money. “Just told it like I saw it, sir.” And he was gone.

I unpacked, poured myself a Bushmills, and sat for a while looking at the schedule of talks looking for some clue as to which ones Galkin might attend. After a while, I decided he wasn't there for the lectures at all. He was there as a cover to meet with people who might reasonably be expected to attend them, or B, to meet with people attending the talks and screw the cover.

He was there for the people. That made me think that the kind of people he was there for would be the kind of people interested in sailing across the North Pole after it melts. That talk was that afternoon after lunch. Or as the brigadier would say, luncheon because lunch is a verb.

I put on a cravat and took the elevator down to the lobby. There I sat and read the *Wall Street Journal* while I watched the ebb and flow of people. I was wondering if Galkin would come down for lunch, and if he did, whether I would be able to pick him out.

He did. He came down, and he had no intention of keeping a low profile. He had the habitual cocaine user's inflated arrogance. He strode out of the elevator with a guy in a suit on his right and a woman with long, natural platinum hair who was almost wearing a skirt trotting behind him. Around them were four guys who looked like they'd fallen out of a Marvel comic. If they'd stood on each other's shoulders, they'd have reached a height of twenty-seven feet easy and a total weight of well over one and a half thousand pounds. Their combined jaws could have stopped tectonic plates from shifting. If they'd had brains, they would have been dangerous.

They moved in a brazen band across the lobby to the conference room, where he stopped, issued instructions, and went inside with the guy I'd labeled as his secretary. Two of the hulks moved toward the bar with the girl, and the other two stood near the entrance with their hands clasped in front of them. I dropped the *Journal* on the table beside me, got to my feet, and moved toward the conference.

FIVE

THE FIRST PART OF THE TALK LASTED FORTY-FIVE minutes because apparently that is how long trained modern minds are able to concentrate before their ADHD kicks in. It was more interesting than I had expected, and as we all moved down toward the coffee and cookies, I scanned the crowd for Galkin. I eventually saw him a few bodies ahead of me chatting with a man and a woman as they shuffled toward the table laid with a white linen cloth and manned by waiters in extremely long aprons.

He told the guy, "Champagne," and I stood beside him. "Make that two."

He glanced at me like I might be crowding his space. I smiled and said, "Who'd have thought, just five thousand miles from Russia to the Western Sahara and Mauritania, and seven thousand to Colombia. It seems we are entering a new world."

We took our glasses and as we turned away, he said, "You're in shipping?"

I made a small wince, then gave a small laugh. "I have things shipped, and I am always interested in exploring alternative routes."

He laughed. "You have things shipped? Is that deliberately cryptic?"

I shrugged and spread my hands. "Eight billion people all around the globe, and every one of them wants something. Some want a bowl of rice, others want a golden statue of themselves, some want coke or heroin, a lot want oil, and many, many of them want guns." He stopped and turned to face me, watching, listening. I held his eye a moment, like I was reading him. "And you know the darnedest thing? Everybody has a moral view on what everybody else wants. And what's worse, everybody has a law about what everybody else can buy or sell. It makes having certain products shipped more difficult every day, if you try to stay within the law."

"I didn't catch your name," he said like he hadn't heard a word I'd said.

"Mitch," I said, using the name the brigadier and I had agreed on the night before. "Mitch Carlisle."

I was about to reach out my hand and ask his name but he said, "Do you know who I am?"

I made a face like I had put my foot in it and said, "Don't tell me. You are somehow involved in making or enforcing the laws that regulate shipping routes."

He arched an eyebrow. "Not exactly. Mr. Carlisle, I don't think I have seen you around before."

"Nope. I avoid these events, and I do ninety percent of my business on the phone."

"But you're here today because...?"

"I am fishing on behalf of my principal."

"What are you fishing for?" I made another kind of wince, but before I could answer, he raised his index finger. "But no, before you tell me, let us cut through some of the bullshit. You say you do not know who I am, yet you place yourself next to me at the refreshments, you initiate a conversation and move swiftly and directly into a subject matter which you treat as though it were risky, yet you are very careless about." He gestured at me. "You yourself said I might have been a government official. Your approach was amateur, Mr. Carlisle, and I ask you again. Do you know who I am?"

I affected embarrassment. I have seen it in other people so I know what it looks like. Then I took a deep breath and said, "Okay, you're right, I am an amateur. I said as much. But to answer your question, no. I have no idea who you are."

"Then why the charade, Mr. Carlisle? I warn you I am running short of patience."

"I am a kind of broker. I deal with a small client base, but we move very large sums of money. We sail pretty close to the line sometimes, but we keep it legal—almost always. You may not believe it, but though I rarely get out of my office, through the Internet and the trade press, I am familiar with all the major players. So when I got here, I knew I was looking for a person who would fit my bill for the deal I need to do. And I thought it might be you."

He frowned like he wasn't sure whether to get mad or not. "Me? Why?"

I smiled with little humor. "Your four goons, the way you moved across the lobby, the guys who show up with your cars. You're a big player, the real deal, but I have never seen you in the trade papers or in any of the relevant literature on or off-line. So I figured maybe, just maybe, you might be interested in dealing with my principal."

He took a deep breath and sighed. "Mr. Carlisle, I—"

"We are talking about seven hundred and fifty million dollars. Bank transfer from Panama to any account you name."

His eyebrows slid down, and his mouth closed slowly. "Seven hundred and fifty million US dollars?"

"I told you we are a small, select group, and we move very large sums of money. Now I need to ask you a question. Was I wrong about you? Did I assess you correctly? If I was wrong, I'm just here pulling your leg. But if the display in the lobby is for real and you are the real deal, maybe we could talk business."

He pointed at me. "You came here to this event today on the *off chance* that you would find—"

I cut him short, and suddenly my face was serious. "I didn't come here on the off chance. One of my principals told me there was a chance I would meet the kind of dealer I was looking for here. He tends to know what he's talking about, I don't question him, and we keep everything compartmentalized. If you are not interested in exploring this further, I have clearly made a mistake, and you'll forgive my sense of humor—"

"Wait." He raised a hand. "You have to be careful in this business. Can you prove any of this?"

I laughed an amiable laugh. "I don't need to prove a damned thing to you. Especially as I don't even know your name yet. All I need to do is transfer three quarters of a billion dollars into an account of your choosing. Will that be proof enough?"

He held out his hand. "Nick Galkin. Like you, I keep a low profile, even if I live large at times. Mr. Carlisle, if we are going to do business, there are a few things I need to know. The first of them is whether I have access to the product you want."

I spread my hands. "Can I suggest we go somewhere more private?" I grinned. "I could use a man's drink, anyway."

He didn't show any sign of finding the comment amusing. He studied my face for a fraction of a second, nodded once, and said, "Wait here."

I watched him cross the room to where the guy I'd pegged as his assistant was talking to a small group of men. They were the kind of men whose egos were permanently attached like balloons to the hot air pumps of their country clubs. They exchanged words, took their leave of the inflated egos, and moved through the crowd to join me where I was waiting. Galkin gestured to his man and said, "Urquhart, Ian. He is my lawyer and advisor. We'll go to the bar, and you can give us a little more detail. We'll take it from there."

I smiled and nodded at Urquhart. "How do you do?"

He didn't smile back. He said, "I do all right."

He had a soft brogue, and I pegged him as Edinburgh. He obviously didn't care how I did.

We followed Galkin out of the lecture hall. His two gorillas fell into step behind us, and we crossed the lobby into the bar. I was surprised when he spotted his girlfriend sitting, laughing with her two gorillas and crossed the room to join her. He jerked his head at the apes, and all four of them left the bar. Galkin sat beside his lady, who had eyes of a startling deep blue, and gestured for me and Urquhart to sit.

Urquhart sat. I didn't. "Is the lady to be part of this conversation?"

"Yes. She is a part of all my conversations. Is that going to be a problem?"

I shook my head. "No."

The waiter showed, we gave him our orders, and he went away. Galkin spread his hands. "So what are you buying, Mr. Carlisle?"

I made a show of trying not to make a show of hesitating. I stared hard at the girl, who stared hard back with her astonishing eyes. I glanced at Urquhart and finally fixed my eyes on Nick Galkin.

"Weapons."

He laughed out loud. Urquhart laughed too, but it was a small, nerdy, patronizing laugh. The girl just smiled. I kind of sighed a smile and placed my hands on my knees like I was about to stand.

"I'm sorry," I said. "It looks as though I am wasting your time and was about to waste my principal's money."

As I went to stand, he raised a hand. "Please, Mr. Carlisle, forgive me. Forgive us. Please sit and enjoy your whiskey with us. We are not laughing at you. But..." He shrugged and gestured at me with his open palm. "All of this to buy arms? Your principal can buy arms anywhere."

"How do you know?"

He frowned. "Excuse me?"

I raised my eyebrows and my voice just a little. "How do you know? You were laughing at a joke without a punch line because you didn't listen to the end. You don't know who my principals are. So how can you know where they can buy arms—or indeed *if* they can buy arms? And you don't know what kind of weapons they want to buy. So again, you can't know where or if they can buy them." I fixed him hard with my eye and said very deliberately, "If you're going to be a put-down merchant, Mr. Galkin, you need to improve your timing."

Silences can have characters all their own. This was a very angry one. I bit into it with my next words and said, "Are you interested in discussing seven hundred and fifty million dollars' worth of business, Mr. Galkin?"

He drew breath to answer, but on an impulse, I leaned across to the girl, who was watching me like a cat watching a mouse hole. I held her eye for a long two seconds and said, "I am not afraid of your goons, and I do not like being patronized." Then I looked up at Galkin. "Can we talk business or are we done?"

He blinked slowly and suppressed a sigh of anger. "What kind of weapons are you interested in, Mr. Carlisle?"

I held up three fingers and showed them to him. I paused while the waiter showed up and distributed our drinks. As he walked away, I said, "We are interested in three categories of weapon that all come under one umbrella: technologically cutting edge. We are interested in biological and chemical, we are very interested in nuclear, and we are especially interested in technological weapons systems that allow you a three hundred and sixty degree *global* control of the battlefield."

He was frowning hard. "Holy shit! That is a tall order. Who the hell is your principal?"

"Please notice, Mr. Galkin, that I am not throwing my head back and busting my sides laughing. My principals are people who can afford to spend a billion dollars on getting exactly and precisely what they want."

I wasn't all that surprised when Galkin's girlfriend answered.

"You made your point, Carlisle, or whatever your name is. Three general categories. How about some more detail? There are prototype jets that would get through seven hundred million pretty fast."

"Yeah?" I laughed obnoxiously. "And how many of those can you lay your hands on by Tuesday, sister?"

She didn't answer. "I can show you a shopping list, but it's flexible. I don't know if you're getting this, but what my principal is interested in is the technology. The next battlefield we fight in will be controlled by artificial intelligence. We are especially interested in weapons that are beginning to incorporate this." I gave a humorless smile. "G.I. Bot. We want to get him, clone him, and try him out."

Something about the way I said it made Galkin frown again. "Try him out? Where?"

"That's need to know. Like I said. I can give you a shopping list. But if, based on that, you want to make offers or suggestions, we are open to that too."

He shook his head. "I have never seen an offer like this before."

I didn't hesitate. "And you'll never see one again, I shouldn't wonder. Have you ever seen the world in this state before? Right now, everything is up for grabs, Galkin. The world you see today will be gone in ten years, and what will be left in its place is anybody's guess." I pointed at him, right at his face. "The guy with the money, who knows how to use that money, will be the most powerful man on the planet."

He gave his head a twitch. "You talk big, mister."

"Yeah, that's because I am paying big, too. All you have to do is produce the goods, guarantee delivery, and watch that money go into your account. Can you do it or are we just pissing in the wind here?"

It was unconscious, and he caught himself as soon as he'd done it, but not soon enough to hide it. He glanced at the woman. She ignored him. He said, "Yeah, we can do it."

"How soon?"

She arched an eyebrow. "You're in a hurry?"

I didn't flinch. "Yeah. Is that a problem?"

"No." She narrowed her eyes. "But why the hurry?"

I smiled at her. "That's none of your beeswax, sweetheart. We're in a hurry, and we are ready to pay. If you can deliver, we have a deal. If you can't, I'll keep looking."

She studied my face nice and slow, and I knew what she was thinking. If my principal was in that much of a hurry for cutting-edge technology, that made him Russian because the whole intelligence community knew that the Western moratorium on arming Ukraine was about to end. The States and Britain had screwed every last concession they could get out of Volodymyr Zelenskyy. They now owned the breadbasket of Europe, and they were going to defend it with everything they had.

They had also lured a bankrupt Russia into racing to rearm by pouring forty percent of its GDP into arms manufacturing, and now they were going to destroy the whole lot. It would be like the road to Basra all over again, only this time it would be the road to Moscow. So Moscow was in a hurry. Which meant I represented Moscow.

She shrugged and looked at Galkin. "We can do that, right, honey?"

"That depends on how much of a hurry you're in."

I had them hooked, and that made me smile. "How fast can you get it?"

I didn't wait for a reply. I drained my glass of whiskey, sighed, and stood. I handed Galkin a card with a cell number on it.

"Call me. I'm in a hurry. Maybe that means my price is negotiable. Maybe it doesn't. But drag your heels and somebody else will fill the bill. If you have something to offer me, make it quick. Otherwise"—I smiled and shrugged—"enjoy the conference."

They didn't call me back this time. I was pretty sure I hadn't overplayed my hand. Just shy of a billion dollars with a hint that the price was negotiable is a hard hand to overplay. Especially if the fish you've hooked believes Moscow might be footing the bill.

I went and had a light lunch, then went up to my suite and made a few preparations. When they were done, I called room service for a couple of bottles of Krug and some Russian caviar. Then I stretched out on the sofa with a whodunit about some gang in the Bronx who were killed playing poker, and the boss had his head and his balls cut off and placed in the middle of the table. It's not enough that it's my job. I have to read about it in my leisure time too.

The call came at nine-thirty p.m. It was the woman.

"Mr. Carlisle, we think we might have a proposal that will interest you."

SIX

I GRUNTED. "NOW, SEE, MAYBE I AM BEING overcautious, but a proposal is not what I asked you guys for. I was very precise in what I said. I said—"

"Relax, Mr. Carlisle. It's a figure of speech. We have a list of products we are pretty sure you'll like. We can guarantee delivery along a secure route—we specialize in that—and shipping will be prompt. Again, we have a reputation in the trade, and that is not something we want to jeopardize."

"That sounds better than a proposal. When can I see it?"

"In the next half hour. You want to come to—"

"No. Sorry." I gave an apologetic laugh. "Aside from having an overactive survival instinct, I also have some software set up in my suite that means payment can only be made from here, while my principal is watching the transaction. On the plus side, it also means guaranteed, instantaneous payment for you. Let me stress, Miss, ahh..."—I waited, but she didn't say anything—"that if this deal is successful, we will be keen to repeat it."

"That sounds good to me. So shall we come to you in half an hour?"

"Please do. I have some Russian caviar and a couple of bottles of Krug on ice."

"I could end up liking you, Mr. Carlisle."

"The feeling is mutual, Miss Noname."

She giggled and hung up.

They showed up thirty-five minutes later, Nick Galkin at the front, the nameless wonder hanging on his arm in a gold satin dress that clung to her like it never wanted to let go, Ian Urquhart, clutching an attaché case, just behind his right shoulder and surrounding them four giants in Italian suits. Each one of them had a sign that said *Russian Special Forces* where his face should have been.

I grinned at Galkin. "What fun. I didn't realize you were bringing the whole family."

He didn't answer, so I stood back and waved them in. Urquhart, Galkin, and the girl took their seats in the sitting area. The big gorillas made like redwoods and stood at the four corners of the room.

"I have some champagne on ice and some caviar. I hope you will join me. But shall we dispose of business first?"

It was Galkin who answered, "Let's do that."

He gave Urquhart the nod. Urquhart put the leather case on the coffee table and opened it. I sat. The screen was a deep burgundy with a blue emblem showing an eagle above two crossed swords. Below the emblem were the words *True Blue Security*, and beneath that, *Peace through Strength*.

Urquhart started talking, as though by rote.

"We can provide you with any conventional weapons on the market today, at competitive prices, but most important, we can deliver them without infringing any international laws or embargos, anywhere on the planet you like. Anything from AK47s and HK416s to tanks, fighters, and bombers. Obviously, there are certain aircraft, like the Grumman B-2, that are not available on the market. Only twenty-one of those were ever built, and they all belong to the United States government. But there are a lot of highly advanced aircraft available on the market."

I looked at Galkin. "Is this going somewhere?"

"Yes. Listen."

He spoke for another ten minutes about what was available and what wasn't. It turned out just about everything was available if you had a few hundred million to spend. It was just the real cutting-edge, high-tech space age stuff that the Pentagon kept for itself.

Then something about the way he paused and said, "However" made me sit up and pay attention.

"It's a fact," he said, "that much of the United States' most advanced armored vehicles and jets actually date, in their original designs, back to the seventies and eighties. By then, there was nothing left to learn about aerodynamics, traction, or suspension. Any improvements that were to be made to vehicles of war would be, to some extent, in materials, but above all in software. Radar, infrared cameras, tracking, targeting, lasers—all of these areas have developed well beyond what the general public realizes, and all of these advances can be fitted to hardware that was designed and developed between the mid-seventies and the early to mid-nineties."

He paused and looked at me with an expression that was close to contempt and strangely at odds with what he said.

"Two 2006 F-35s might cost you close to five hundred million dollars and would be awkward to transport and highly visible. But with the right technological upgrades, you can take your existing 1976 Falcon, upgrade its software and weapons systems, reduce its RCS—that is its radar cross section—by using RAMs—that is, radar absorbing materials—and turn it into a space age killing machine.

"It need hardly be said that the transport and delivery of this technology is much easier and more discreet than transporting entire planes."

I raised my right hand, and he paused the presentation video.

"Wait a second, what exactly are you proposing here? You want me to spend close to a billion dollars on software?"

Galkin glanced at Urquhart and gave him an almost imperceptible nod. Then he turned to me.

"I assume you have heard of the Rat Labs in New Mexico."

"Of course."

"Did you know they have a second lab in Mexico itself?"

I stared at him for a long moment and said, "No" like I didn't believe him.

He shrugged. "Sinaloa, close to the border with Durango." He laughed. "You see it from the air, or a satellite, hey! It's some poor guy's dilapidated farm. But look a bit closer." He frowned. "Huh! That guy can land a couple of choppers in his land, in that meadow. And that road, that road that seems to go nowhere, could that be a runway? Yes." He nodded. "I have been there. They have no need for major transportation because most of their work is in IT and artificial intelligence. The really good stuff goes to..." He trailed off and shrugged. "It goes to a select group based partly at the Pentagon whose interest lies, among other things, in preserving the military superiority of the United States. But the second-rate stuff—which is damned good!— gets sold, with some modifications, to anyone who can afford it."

Urquhart reached in the top of the attaché case and pulled out a sheaf of glossy pages. As he handed them to me, Galkin started talking again.

"I am going to show you a series of videos now, Mr. Carlisle. As you watch them, I want you to be aware of something. Ninety-nine percent of my clients get what's on the market, and they come to me because I have a network that guarantees delivery, and timely delivery. One percent or less get access to the Sinaloa Rat labs. You're going to see why." He pointed at the glossy pages in my hand. "Those are the stats of these machines."

I was then treated to forty-five minutes of an orgy of speed, maneuverability, precision targeting, and sheer power that I had to admit was impressive. What he had said was true. The war machines designed from the '70s to the '90s were, in terms of design, as good as it gets. What had improved since then were, to some extent, the materials—particularly stealth materials—computerization, and battlefield artificial intelligence. What I was seeing on the screen was how forty- and fifty-year-old machines with upgrades in technology could lay waste to all but the most advanced Western weaponry.

When the show was over, I made a show of being mad and trying to control it. I dropped the pages on the table and stared at Galkin for a moment.

"This is not what I was expecting."

He sat forward with his elbows on his knees. "It is a damn sight better than what you were expecting, Carlisle, and you know it." He looked at Urquhart and held out his hand. Urquhart handed him a slim sheaf of printed papers. He showed it to me. "This is my offer."

I looked it over. It was a breathtaking array of cutting-edge technologies, including biochemical weapons, that could turn a small, moderately efficient army into a lethal war machine. I ran my fingers through my hair and sighed. Galkin threw his hands in the air.

"You know what I think your problem is, Carlisle? You're afraid to show this to your principal because it is not what he asked for. But let me tell you something. Let me tell you this: I have a hunch I know who your principal is, and when he sees this, he'll be doing cartwheels. This is game-changing technology for anyone who uses it. And only a select few get to even see it!"

I glanced over at my own laptop sitting on the desk in the corner. I hesitated a moment, then stood. "Please, give me a moment."

I went into the bedroom, pulling out my cell. I closed the door, photographed the six pages and sent them to the brigadier, then phoned him.

"Yes."

"Sir, you have seen their offer. It is not what you asked me for. I felt sure this morning..."

"It's good. It's much better than I expected. Get assurances of delivery and pay them."

"But sir..."

"Do it!"

He hung up. I didn't know if they were listening or not, but if they were, I rated it a pretty good performance. I waited a couple of minutes and returned to the main room. I closed the bedroom door behind me and stood looking down at Galkin.

"What guarantees of delivery can you offer?"

The girl smiled. Galkin said, "Surprisingly enough, that is about the easiest part of all. My business relies on two things above all else: my reputation, through which I ensure the good will of my clients, both buyers and sellers, and my legal status. Legally I sail very, very close to the wind, and I *never* let myself get caught crossing the line." He spread his hands and shrugged. "Look at me! I am a respected man who moves freely about the world without fear of lawsuits or prosecution. My clients like that, and so do I. Now you tell me, think it through, Carlisle, if I fail to deliver on seven hundred and fifty million dollars' worth of goods, what will happen to my reputation? Not only that, what will your principal, a man of considerable means, do to me?" He laughed. "I would be lucky if he only ruined me financially. He would make an example of me, and quite rightly so." He extended a hand toward me. "Come, let us finalize this deal and enjoy your champagne and caviar. To quote Rick in *Casablanca*, this could be the beginning of a beautiful friendship!"

We spent the next half hour finalizing a form of words, printing up documents, and signing them. When we were done, I got my laptop, opened up the page with our Panama digital bank account, typed in the amount to pay as $750,000,000 and set the laptop on the table for them to see. The girl took a deep breath and smiled. Galkin glanced at her, and I caught something in his eyes like hope. Urquhart looked like he might pee in his pants. I clicked okay, and the money sent. I logged out and closed the laptop. Meanwhile, Urquhart rattled at his own keyboard, sat a moment motionless staring at the screen, then smiled and nodded and nodded again at Galkin.

"It's through."

I made a show of allowing myself to relax and smile broadly at Galkin. "Champagne," I said. "I think that was all quite successful. I acted on my principal's instructions, you have your money, we have our armament—champagne and caviar!"

I came back a moment later with the silver tray bearing the ice bucket with the two bottles and four flutes, the dish of caviar, and a basket of crackers. I took one of the bottles and started to remove the foil.

"Gentlemen, lady with no name, you will see in the very near future a shift in the balance of power."

I eased the cork. Galkin laughed and said, "She loves to play games. She is not Russian, like me. She is Norwegian, from the land of the Vikings. You are proud of your heritage, eh, Anni?"

She didn't look at him. She was watching me. She said, "I admire the Vikings. They took what they wanted and conquered the world. No apologies, no guilt. Just action."

Galkin was grinning, relaxing. He said, "You have not been properly introduced. Anni, meet Mitch Carlisle. Mitch, meet Anniken Larsen."

It was a fraction of a second, but the name caught me by surprise. The cork erupted from the bottle, and I used that to hide it, but as I filled the glasses, I could feel her eyes on me. She had caught it. I smiled at her and handed her a glass as I said, "Anniken."

But in my mind, I was playing the brigadier talking to General Moorcroft, saying, "...Galkin will not be his sole target. He will also eliminate Galkin's personal assistant of the last five years, Anniken Larsen, who is widely tipped to become his heir and successor."

I had assumed Anniken Larsen was a man. Now it was this woman, and I was going to have to kill her. I handed Galkin and Urquhart a glass each and poured my own. I raised my glass.

Galkin and Urquhart raised theirs, but Galkin was watching Larsen, who was watching me and had not raised her glass. She waited till we had drunk before she spoke.

"You know my name," she said.

I offered her a facetious smile and said, "Yup."

"No." She shook her head and looked at her glass on her knee. What there was of a smile had faded. "You knew my name before Nick told you."

Galkin and Urquhart were frowning, looking from Larsen to me and back again. I said, "I'm not following you, Anniken."

She was biting her lip, and her eyes traveled up to the ceiling. "You knew my name, but you didn't know it was me. When Nick told you my name, it surprised you." She turned her head to look at me. "You son of a bitch, you came here looking for us."

I scowled like a man who was offended. "Woah! What's this?" I turned to Galkin. "What game is she playing? I played straight with you. Hell! I just put three quarters of a billion bucks in your account! Now you're going to spring this bullshit on me?"

Galkin turned to Larsen. He was frowning. "What?" he said. "What..."

The four gorillas were looking confused. I stood, muttering about how I didn't have to put up with this crap. I pointed at Larsen. "Did you see the money go into the account? Did you see Ian give Nick the okay? Did you *see* that?"

I grabbed the bucket of ice and the unopened bottle and stormed into the kitchenette. I opened the cutlery drawer and pulled out my suppressed Sig. That was when I heard the crash. I turned and looked. Urquhart had collapsed onto the table. Galkin was lying back, groaning. Anniken Larsen was on her feet, pointing at me and screaming. She was screaming, "*Kill him! Kill him!*"

They weren't confused anymore. They knew exactly what to do.

SEVEN

They were fast. The Russian military is big, clumsy, badly organized, and hampered by excessive bureaucracy. The individuals in their special operations units are recruited for their lack of intelligence and discrimination and their willingness to do anything they are told to do. That and their sheer brute force. They are tough, hard, and unrelenting. And these guys were fast.

The first one barreled through the door scowling like he was real mad, he didn't know why, and he didn't care. I'm fast. I had the Sig leveled at his head, and I was squeezing the trigger. But his huge left hand smashed into my wrist as the weapon spat. The slug hit the wall and showered plaster and concrete over his bald head as he smashed his fist into my face.

I was lucky my arm was in his way, and I weaved back or he would have taken my head off. I stumbled, and his front kick hurled me against the fridge. It had been a glancing blow, but there were needles of pain stabbing through my back, and I knew if his next blow connected, I would be in serious trouble.

His next blow was going to be a stamp with the heel of his patent leather shoe, driven down by three hundred and fifty pounds of solid muscle and stupidity. The stamp was aimed where no guy should ever get stamped on, and his big gorilla face leered down at me like he was saying, "This is really going to hurt!" though what he actually said was, "Zasranets!"

He leered half a second too long, and I shot him in the balls. The look of astonishment on his face turned to horror just before he faded and fell back into his pals, who were rushing in behind him. There was blood gushing down his pants and onto the floor. I struggled back against the fridge, scrambling to get to my feet. His friends pushed him aside and to the floor. The nearest one, younger and leaner than the others, stepped over him and slipped in the blood. He fell against the kitchen table and overturned it as I slid my back up the fridge. The other two had their weapons in their hands, but Anniken was in the door hissing, *"No guns! They will hear us! No guns!"*

There was a pause for a fraction of a second. The thin guy leaned on the table to get up, but his feet kept slipping in the gore on the tiled floor. Anniken leered at me and said, "Strangle him."

The two guys standing rushed me. The guy on my left seized my left arm with hands like vises. He had one big eyebrow and black eyes that stared into mine. The guy on my right, who had giant ears and a moustache, grabbed my gun arm with his left hand and my throat with his right. Anniken was shouting, "I want to see his eyes bulge! I want to see his tongue!"

The pressure on my throat was intense, and I could feel the blood pressure rising in my head. My lungs were screaming for air, and I knew I probably had seconds to live. As he squeezed with his right hand, his left was pushing my gun hand away to my right. I have often said that if somebody is strangling you, and you focus on their hands, you will die. You have to focus on what weapons you have available.

Each tenth of a second was a screaming agony in my lungs, but I bent my wrist, calculated the angle, and pulled the trigger. The slug punched into his thigh. His eyes went wide, and he let go of me and staggered back a step. It was enough for me to bring the Sig across my belly and pump two rounds into Monobrow's chest. In a continuous fluid movement, I put the suppressor to Big Ears' forehead and pumped two rounds into it. They exploded out a hole the size of a large grapefruit in the back of his head and sprayed brains, blood, and gore all over Anniken Larsen's face and cleavage.

For half a second I saw her, a weird expression on her twisted face as she said, "Ah... Ah... Ah..."

But the thin guy was at me, trying to twist the gun out of my hand. He was strong, and I was winded. He pounded at my head with his right fist while trying to twist the barrel of the Sig with his left hand. I managed to lean and weave so half his punches hit the fridge.

I managed to head-butt his chin, but I couldn't get any purchase, so all it did was send him back a couple of paces. But this guy was made of rock, and he came back in swinging right and left hooks to my floating ribs and my head. I did the only thing I could do. I lifted my feet off the floor and dropped. The two punches that were meant to destroy me drove into the steel fridge, and this time, they hurt. I could tell by the way he roared.

He found me on the floor beneath him and drew back his right foot for what would have been a lethal kick. But he was just half a second too late. I already had the Fairbairn and Sykes in my hand, and I drove it deep into his inside thigh, cutting through his femoral vein and artery. For a moment, he did an almost comical imitation of Elvis Presley, only it wasn't funny. It was cruel and ugly. I slid out from under him and pulled the knife from his leg. His blood gushed onto the floor to add to the wash of gore and death that had swamped the kitchenette.

Anniken Larsen was gone. I picked my way over the bodies, trying not to slip and fall, and found her in the living room, still covered in gore, gathering up Urquhart's attaché case with the laptop in it. Galkin was still stretched out, but now instead of groaning, he was snoring. Urquhart had slipped from the table onto the floor, and he was snoring too. Anniken pointed a trembling finger at me.

"Don't come near me! Don't come near me or I'll scream!"

"Okay."

She scrambled over to Galkin, dropped the case, and started reaching under his jacket for his piece. I put the Sig in my waistband, stepped over, and grabbed the back of her gold satin dress. It was lower cut at the back than at the front and reached almost down to her ass. I was in pain and pretty mad, so I grabbed, and maybe I pulled too hard, but there was a ripping sound, and the dress came off in my hands, leaving her in a pair of cute pink panties and three-inch heels. The rage on her face was something to see. In a swift movement that took me by surprise, she grabbed the half empty bottle of Krug and backhanded me with it across my head. The pain was excruciating, like someone had hammered a knitting needle through my skull, and for a couple of seconds, I blacked out. In the blackness I heard a weird scream and felt a sharp, stabbing pain in my leg.

The door slammed, and I struggled out of the blackness and sat up. There was an ugly, heel-shaped hole in my trouser leg, smeared with blood. I levered myself to my feet, pulled the Sig from my waistband behind my back, and finished Galkin and Urquhart, then I called the brigadier.

"News?"

"Yeah... Anniken Larsen is a woman. We are going to need some serious housekeeping, and I might need a doctor. I think I have a concussion, not just in my head but everywhere."

There was silence for a short while. Then he said, "They're on their way. Are you okay?"

"A naked Anniken Larsen just hit me with a bottle of Krug. I'm not sure if it was half empty or half full. Did you *know* she was a woman? And my kitchen is full of dead men and blood."

"I'm on my way. I'll get you out of there."

"Yeah, thanks."

I hung up, went to the bathroom, and vomited a few times.

When I was done, I went to the bedroom and started packing my stuff. That was when I wasn't trying to hold the room steady. I spent a while doing that at the closet, holding the door to stop the room moving. I was wondering if I could make it to the bathroom to be sick.

I tried, but my feet didn't get the memo, and the floor came up and smacked me in the face. I have a vague recollection of the brigadier looking at me through the darkness and saying, "Don't look in the mirror," and some guy with a syringe chuckling. It wasn't a cruel chuckle, but it was a chuckle. Then there was blessed oblivion.

When I awoke, I was in my old room at Cobra HQ. Judging by the light coming through the window, the wafting curtains, and the sounds coming from the apple orchard, I figured it was midmorning. I levered myself onto one elbow and made the room rock gently. When it stopped, I made my way to the bathroom and spent a while being ill and feeling sorry for myself. I did that again only with more feeling after I looked in the mirror. The left side of my face looked like somebody had put a bicycle pump in it and inflated it, then painted it purple after sticking a mutilated plum where my left eye should be. No wonder Anniken had screamed and fled. The Thing from the Black Lagoon had just ripped her dress off.

Then I remembered a good part of the ugly purple swelling was probably caused by her deft use of Mjöllnir, the Krug Bottle.

I pulled on the fresh clothes that had been left for me on the chair and made my way carefully downstairs. In the quiet drawing room, I stopped and looked through the plate glass sliding doors that gave on to the swimming pool. The brigadier was there, sitting at the table in the shade of an umbrella, reading what looked like a report. I felt a stab in my gut. Jane should have been there, ready to give me a hard time and ride me about being a caveman. I wondered if there was any news, if she had died while I was getting seven bales of shit beaten out of me.

I stepped through the door into the sunshine, and the brigadier looked up and smiled.

"You need protein," he said.

"Yeah, I ignored your advice and looked in the mirror. My face has turned into one big subcutaneous hemorrhage."

"We'll soon get you fixed up." He pressed a button on the fob beside him. "The usual eggs, bacon, sausages..."

"All that." I hesitated a moment. "Any news?"

"No change. She is still in intensive care."

"Does that mean she's gone into a coma?"

"Technically, yes. But it's not a deep coma, and I am told there is a good chance she will come out in a day or two."

His mouth said that, but his face said he was lying. I decided to change the subject.

"Did you know Anniken Larsen was a woman?"

"No."

"It came as a shock. Especially as she was coming on to me pretty strong just before I realized I had to kill her."

"I can imagine. Harry, did you remove her dress?" He was frowning and looked worried.

"Not intentionally, no. The dress came off when I tried to stop her shooting me with Galkin's gun. Then she hit me with a half-full bottle of Krug."

He tried to suppress a smile but failed. "You do lead an exciting life, don't you?"

"Yeah, amazing. I got Galkin and Urquhart; what about the virus?"

"We have initial reports from the NSA and GCHQ that suggest his network of offshore accounts and companies have been wiped and are in deep chaos. It will take a few days to confirm it, but that seems to be the case. You did well."

"But I let Anniken Larsen get away. And then there is the issue of the Rat Labs in Mexico, in Sinaloa."

"That's not our bag, Harry. Larsen is, but not the Rat Labs."

I smiled. It was an amiable smile, but God alone knows what

it looked like with my face the way it was. "I don't work for you anymore, remember?"

He nodded. "I remember. I also know you are in no fit condition to set foot out of doors, let alone go hunting femmes fatal and hidden labs."

Behind me and slightly to my left, Jacques, the brigadier's manservant, stepped out with a large tray of various types of protein of the eggs, bacon, and sausages variety, accompanied by a large pot of coffee. I watched him approach a moment and said, "Yeah, well, I haven't had breakfast yet."

He didn't laugh. Neither did I.

THE NEXT TWO or three days were slow and frustrating, but they gave me the chance to recover and for the bruising on my face to die down some. The brigadier avoided me most of the time, and on the few occasions when I managed to collar him, he answered my questions in vague, evasive terms. He told me there was little change in the colonel's condition and investigations into the whereabouts of Anniken Larsen were progressing and satisfactory. The Nick Galkin network of companies and bank accounts appeared to have collapsed in a heap of chaos, if a total absence of anything at all can be called a heap of chaos.

"So what can I be doing? Should I go home?"

He smiled and patted me on the shoulder. "Rest and relax, old friend. Rest and relax. We'll have news soon enough."

And he made his way up the stairs toward his private study, where nobody could get him.

So on day four I went down to the gym and started working out and getting back into shape again. I was slow, things hurt, my muscles told me not to strain so hard, but overall, I wasn't as bad as I thought.

I ate lunch and went back to the gym to do lengths in the indoor pool and a couple of hours with a variety of sacks, practicing kicks and combinations. At six, after a shower and a change of clothes, I was surprised to find the brigadier sitting at the table beside the outdoor pool, reading Lao Tzu's *Art of War*. He looked up and smiled.

"I hope you've made the most of your rest."

I sat and gave my head a twitch of reluctance. "It's hard to make the most of something you don't want."

"Well, you'll be glad to know then that we are on."

"We're on? What does that mean?"

"It means Anniken Larsen has been found."

EIGHT

Jacques emerged from the house with a tray of drinks. He mixed us a couple of martinis and informed us that we would be having tender artichoke hearts with pine nuts dressed with fresh thyme, olive oil from Baena, and lemon juice, followed by tender, diced lamb stir fried in nutmeg and cinnamon on a bed of basmati rice and doused with fresh double cream.

"To accompany the artichokes we eff a light, fruity Pape Clément, and for the lamb we eff a Moillard Nuits Saint George with *suggestion* of cranberry and raspberry which is nice with the lamb."

"That sounds fine, Jacques."

"Twenty minutes." He shrugged and spread his hands. "'Alf an hour?"

He turned and walked away without waiting for a response. I studied the brigadier as he sipped his drink.

"It's like you're celebrating," I said, "but keeping it low key. You have some news."

"Jane has come out of her coma. She is very weak, and we cannot go and see her, and she is not out of the woods yet, but she has woken up."

I nodded and reached for my drink. "A cautious celebration." I raised my glass. "Her good health and rapid recovery."

"Here's to that."

We drank, and I set down my glass. "So what about Anniken Larsen? Where is she?"

He smiled on one side of his face and made it look sad.

"She's in Singapore, at the Raffles, staying in the Palm Court Suite."

"Of course she is."

"You're booked in at the Intercontinental, three hundred and fifty yards away. You'll have to have some form of disguise. The risk of being seen and recognized is too high."

I nodded. "Okay."

"You'll have to improvise and act very swiftly."

"What's she doing in Singapore?"

"We are not sure, but it looks as though she is having meetings with Iranian agents who are probably asking her what happened in London and, perhaps, where their order is. If you remember, Jane was investigating Galkin's meetings with certain Russian, Chinese, and Iranian agents in New York. If orders were placed, those clients will be very unhappy right now."

"So our job might be done for us."

"It might be. But we want to make sure it gets done." He watched me for a moment. "She looks like an angel, Harry, but she is a very evil creature. She and Galkin caused a lot of death and unimaginable suffering."

"I know. I'll do it."

"Be careful. You are very good at what you do, Harry, but this woman is like nothing any of us have faced before. She is subtle in the extreme. She was right there, in full view, and managing to deflect suspicion away from herself and on to the men in his retinue. We had no idea until you told us that she was a woman."

I nodded. "I am aware how dangerous she is, sir. When do I go?"

He took a deep breath and drummed his fingers on the table.

"Harry, you know that I have absolute confidence in you, and you would be my first choice for any mission."

I narrowed my eyes at him. "What's that supposed to mean?"

"I had a meeting with the Cobra Council today. I can't tell you who they are, as you well know, but a couple of them are concerned."

"What about?"

He held my eye for a long moment. "I need you to understand that I do not agree with them, Harry."

"What are they concerned about?"

"They are making an issue of the fact that the colonel was injured, possibly fatally, while you were extracting her..."

"I was not part of her mission. She called me in the middle of the night, and I had to improvise as best I could. It's a miracle either of us got out of there alive. And the fact is *both* of us got out alive!"

My voice had been rising. He held my eye throughout. When I'd finished, he said, "I know, Harry. And what you have just told me is what I told them, only I told them in stronger terms. But at the moment, they are not listening. They also point to the fact that Anniken Larsen penetrated your cover. They are saying both incidents happened within a short time of each other, and they are questioning the confidence I have in you."

"Son of a bitch." I said it quietly and looked away. When I looked back, I asked him, "So I am off the case?" I made a gesture you might describe as helpless. "What was the point of all this healing and briefing—"

He blinked once and said, "Harry, stop." I stopped. "Now listen very carefully to me. I run Cobra. I used to run it with Jane's help. Now and for the foreseeable future, I run it on my own. The council gets involved once in a blue moon, usually if something goes wrong. Because it would be catastrophic if it ever came out that the Five Eyes nations run what is effectively a hit squad. So they stay as uninvolved as they possibly can."

I was frowning. "What are you telling me, sir?"

"You cannot figure on any internal documents. You resigned. You came back briefly as a freelancer, and now the council has said they want you off the job. So any internal documents will refer to you as 'the Operative.' I will provide you with whatever support and contacts I can. But to all intents and purposes, you are a rogue operative, and, frankly, so am I."

He paused a moment in thought. When he spoke again, his voice was quiet and he avoided my eye.

"We both care for Jane, Harry. This job is as much revenge as anything else. If anybody is going to do it, it will be you and me."

It was as close as I had ever seen him get to expressing an emotion, and I had no idea how to respond. After a moment, he said, gazing over at the pool,

"How *did* Anniken penetrate your cover?"

I sighed and shook my head, remembering. "I was opening a bottle of Krug. Up to that point, she had avoided giving me her name, and I called her No Name. Galkin introduced her just as the cork popped from the bottle. I used that to cover my surprise. It must have been a fraction of a second, but she caught it. I had smeared the inside of the glasses with curare, but she didn't drink her champagne. She didn't stop Galkin or Urquhart drinking either. She just sat and watched me." I frowned, trying to remember. "She said, 'You know my name.' Then she said, 'You knew my name before Nick told you.' I made like I didn't know what she was talking about and I was getting mad. And she said"—I closed my eyes and thought—"'You knew my name, but you didn't know it was me. When Nick told you my name, it surprised you.' Then she said, "You son of a bitch, you came here looking for us.'"

"And she deduced all of that from the momentary, involuntary contraction of your facial muscles when you heard her name." He studied my face a moment. "She is a very brilliant, dangerous woman, Harry. But I have to tell you there are a couple of members of the council who believe you might have turned. That she might have turned you."

"Who?"

He gave his head a shake that was barely perceptible. Then he looked past me. "Ah," he said. "The artichoke hearts."

When we had been served our food and wine and Jacques had left us to it, the brigadier said, "You'll be taken home tomorrow morning. At some point during the afternoon, you'll receive an Amazon delivery with everything we have on Anniken Larsen, which is precious little, your new passport and driver's license, and your hotel booking. After that, I am afraid you are pretty much on your own." He gave a small shrug and smiled at me. "But then that is pretty much true of every job you have ever done for me, in Cobra or in the Regiment."

"Okay." I nodded.

"But, Harry, if you get stuck, call me. You have my number. I will also give you the number of a contact in Singapore who can provide you with hardware if you need it."

"Thank you."

We ate in silence as evening crept into the darkness of night. When Jacques had taken away the plates and the white wine and replaced them with the lamb and red wine, the brigadier started a desultory kind of broken dialogue, touching on small details of the job I was going to do—the need for some kind of disguise that was not excessive or cumbersome, the best place for the execution, whether it was best for me to contact her openly or seize the advantage of surprise.

Over sheep's cheese, espresso, and twenty-one-year-old Bushmills, he finally said, "Jane is here." I stared at him. "She has a room upstairs and the very best medical care."

"What if—"

"There is no what if. They have done everything they can do. She will either pull through or she won't. The surgeon agreed that her best chance of recovery would be in a place she considered home, with the lawns and the orchards..."

He trailed off. I had half expected him to include himself in the list of things that would help her recover.

"How long has she been here?"

"Since early this morning."

"Why didn't you tell me?"

He held my eye a moment, then smiled. "Because she needed to rest, and so did I. And you needed to be focused on training and recovering. That was the judgment I made. When you have finished your drink, you can go and see her. She wants to see you."

I drained my glass and went to find Jane.

SHE WAS awake when I opened the door and went in. She was pale, and the skin under her eyes was dark. Her mouth smiled, but her eyes were tired, and there was sadness in them. She reached out her hand to me. I took it and sat on the edge of the bed.

"They tried to scare me, telling me you'd look really rough. But I knew you'd look great."

She didn't laugh. She let her thumb stroke the back of my hand. "You're a terrible liar, Harry." I was trying to think of something clever to say, but I saw a tear run down her cheek. She met my eye. "I am so sorry, Harry. I was so stupid and unprofessional. I put your life at risk..."

"Jane, you are the most professional person I know. You took a risk because you knew how high the stakes were. And people like you and me, and the brigadier, we have these jobs because we don't leave the risk-taking to other people. We face the barrel of the gun and we take the risk.

"And let me tell you something else. If you hadn't called me, I would have been so mad at you. I drive you nuts, you drive me nuts, but you and me are pals, and we both know we will always be there for each other. Right?"

The tears were flowing freely now, but there was also a glimmer of a smile in her eyes.

"So let me tell you this, Jane, and nobody on this planet is better placed than me to know this: Everything you did, every step of the way, you did the right thing."

She rested her cheek against my hand and closed her eyes. I dried her cheeks with the corner of her duvet and spoke softly. "You keep fighting there, Jane. You never give up. Hang in there..."

But by then she was snoring softly with just a trace of a smile. I gave her a gentle kiss on the forehead and left the room.

NINE

We touched down at Changi International Airport on the western extreme of Singapore at nine in the morning. Once through passport control and baggage claim, I spent twenty minutes getting my car. The closest thing they had to a decent vehicle was a Maserati GT with four hundred and fifty horses all working hard to make the driver feel safe and relaxed. I slung my luggage in the trunk and took the East Coast Park Road east into town.

Singapore is not a place I know well, but the times I have been there, it has struck me as a mellow form of Hong Kong. It is a place of strange juxtapositions. A little less than a third of the population is Buddhist, and the other two-thirds are a mix of Christians, Hindus, Taoists, and Muslims, and all of them coexist peacefully in one of the three safest cities in the world, an island-city which is driven by a powerful, ambitious market economy and sports some of the most striking sci-fi architecture on the planet.

I crossed the Marina Bay and entered in among the gleaming towers of steel and glass and proceeded among abundant trees and parks to the four-lane highway of Rochor Road. And with a strange feeling I might have slipped into a parallel universe where

Star Trek has played out as reality, after a couple of minutes, I turned left onto Northbridge Road and then ducked into the Inter Continental.

I had made a point of sleeping for most of the flight. It's about the best way to beat the jetlag, and there were things I wanted to do on arrival. So I checked in and had a quick shower to wash the flight and the sleep out of my muscles. After that, I put on a wig of abundant black hair and a beard and moustache that covered most of my face. Then I changed into a linen suit and a pair of shoes that added a good inch to my height and stepped out into the bright, tropical sunshine.

I took a stroll down Victoria Street among the shade of the abundant trees in the gardens that lined the sidewalks and the central reservation. At Cashin Street, a short, twisting alley, I crossed the avenue and made my way down to the Raffles Hotel. It's the kind of building you have to stop and look at. It is only three stories in height, but it has a massive feel to it, and it reeks of the substance of a time when things were made to last and elegance was more important than cost-effectiveness.

My plan, such as it was, was to sit in the lobby for as long as it took and see if she showed up and see who she had with her. It wasn't much of a plan, but it was the best I could improvise, and it was something I could build on. If I could tail her for a day or two, I could find out what kind of security she had and where and when she was vulnerable.

I spent an hour in the vast, white Grand Lobby under the galleried landings and the giant, sparkling chandelier. People came and went. Nobody seemed to notice me. I turned the pages of the *International Herald Tribune* and read the articles for the third time. There was no sign of Anniken Larsen.

At twelve noon, I set down the paper and strolled into the Long Bar. There I picked a table by the window where the light would be behind me and cast my face in shadow and ordered a dry martini.

She came in half an hour later. I almost didn't recognize

her. She was in jeans and a black University of Oslo sweatshirt with a big, red emblem on it and her hair pulled back in a ponytail. She was alone and sat at a table sideways to me, reading what looked like a file. The waiter approached, and she ordered a Diet Coke and returned to her reading. This was a very different Anni than the one I'd met in New York. For a moment I toyed with the idea of going over. With a Sig Sauer pointed at her belly, it wouldn't be hard to convince her to come with me. But caution and common sense told me to wait and observe.

Caution and common sense proved to be right. After fifteen minutes, two men entered the bar down the spiral staircase. They were in their forties and had round, Slavic faces that looked like they'd been left freezing on the Steppes so long they'd forgotten how to make expressions. One of them was bald. The other had thin, sandy hair. They joined her at her table. None of them said anything until she'd put down her file and the waiter had arrived. They were having fun, deep-down fun, where it's not like fun anymore.

I heard the bald one say, "Wodka" in a voice like a geothermal disturbance, and the waiter went away.

The guy with sandy hair said, "Where is product? You are here"—he gestured across the table with his open hand—"with two arms, two legs, two..."—he sneered—"because you agree to meeting. Otherwise maybe you are a bit here, a bit there..."

She leaned forward with her elbows on her knees and spoke quietly, but I just caught her words.

"Threaten me one more time, Ivan, and I will shoot your dick off right here where we are sitting. You want your product. I want you to have your product. I am solving it. Now do you want to talk or do you want to show me how big your Russian dick is?"

I was grateful of the big beard and moustache that hid my grin. The guy, who might have been called Ivan, spluttered. I heard him say, "Zasranets!" as he made to stand. The bald guy put a hand on his shoulder. "Ivan, not now."

Anniken was still leaning forward, staring at Ivan, but now she was smiling. She said in a stage whisper, "Ya tebya kastriruyu."

So far she had called him an asshole and now told him she was going to castrate him. There was no denying she was gutsy, but I couldn't help wondering what she had in the way of backup. The bald guy put a hand on her shoulder too.

"Enough, please, we have business to resolve. When we are done, you can fight all you want. But now business."

The waiter brought a bottle of vodka and three glasses. When he'd gone, Sandy Hair said, "What about product?"

She sighed like she still hadn't made up her mind how much to tell.

"We were attacked with a virus. It did a lot of damage to our records. We are in the process of tracking down all our clients' shipments—"

Ivan broke in. "We don't give fuck 'bout other clients' shipments. Where is *our* product?"

The contempt on her face was not theatrical. It was genuine. "If you'll keep your mouth shut long enough to give your ovaries a rest, I'll tell you."

The language had obviously gotten a little sophisticated for him because he looked at his pal, jerked his chin, and shrugged, which obviously meant, "What?"

His pal said, "Don't talk." To Anniken, he said, "You give our product maximum priority. How long?"

"It is somewhere between Cabinda-Itumba—"

"Where?"

"The west coast of Africa, the Congo, Madagascar, and Victoria Island in the Bay of Bengal. We have agents tracing it as we speak. As soon as we have found it, it is simply a matter of proving ownership and you have your product, Vlad."

The guy called Vlad nodded three times more slowly than you'd think possible. Then he said, "Simply."

Anniken was not a woman to stay very long on the defensive. She gave him the dead eye for a long two seconds and said, "It's not complicated, Vlad. Even Ivan here could do it if he took his finger out of his ass long enough. But I'll tell you what I would like to know. Who the hell attacked us with that virus? Was it you?"

"Of course not."

"There is no 'of course' about it. I can think of several motives right here and now, and the strongest is that once you have your big, hairy hands on that product, you don't want us selling it to anybody else. Give me one good reason why I should not run with that theory."

Vlad's voice was dangerous when he answered. "You do not want to make enemies of Russia—"

"Maybe I do and maybe I don't." She cut him short. "But you and your pet orangutan keep your dicks in your pants and stop the tough guy act. I'm getting tired of your threats. We are finding your product. As soon as we have it, we will forward it to you. Meantime, relax."

Vlad sighed the way an angry bull might. "This is words. You cannot telephone the captain of the ship, you cannot telephone the shipping company..." He spread his hands and shrugged. "This is so hard to believe."

"Okay." She nodded. "You take me. I'll go quietly. You take me where—to the Johor River? Rape me? Shoot me? Or do you make an example of me and torture me first? Then you dump my body in the river." She spread her own hands in a small echo of Vlad's gesture a moment before. "So what happens then, Vlad? Apart from the best assassins in the private sector going after you, Ivan, and Boris himself and causing you very painful deaths, you and Boris can say goodbye to the product forever. It will never be found, and the company will never sell to you again. We have exclusive access to the Works, and we will never trade with you again." She pointed at the bottle. "We going to drink that trash or are you boys going to take it up to your room and have a private party?"

Vlad did his nodding thing again. "Okay," he said. "Now you

have the ace. But if this situation continues more than few days, it will be diminishing return. You do not want this. You do not want play with Russia."

She pushed her glass at him. "Russia can kiss my ass. By the weekend, you'll have your product sitting in Palau Brani. Now stop beating your chest and pour me a fucking drink."

I let them down a couple of vodkas, then rose and left discretely.

Outside, I ducked down Bain Street to Victoria Street, where I stopped and sat on a stone bench outside St Joseph's Church. There I watched the passersby for ten minutes until I was satisfied I was not being followed. Then I pulled out the cell the brigadier had given me and pressed one.

"Yes."

"I found it where we expected to find it."

"And?"

"They had a get-together."

"She and who else?"

"Thirty years ago, I would have said ex-KGB."

"Did you catch any names?"

"Yeah: Ivan, who had no hair and Vlad, who had just a little and sandy. These guys were worried, borderline mad, that what they had ordered had not been delivered."

There was a smile in his voice when he asked, "What did she tell them?"

"She said they'd been hit by a virus which had screwed up their system, but they were on the case, and the goods would show up in a couple of days."

"Did she have any idea where it was?"

"Yup, between Cabinda-Itumba and Victoria Island in the Bay of Bengal."

"Point of departure?"

"She didn't say, but my guess is it originated in North Sinaloa at the Rat Labs there, went by road to Heroica Veracruz or

Altamira on the Gulf, and from there by container through the Caribbean toward Africa."

"We can work with that. Any idea what the order was?"

I thought about it. "He called it a product. It's big enough that it gets shipped rather than carried in a suitcase. And another point I have to mention: when she got mad she mentioned that the end user was Boris. I don't think there is enough data to reach an informed conclusion, but my gut disagrees with my brain. I think we are talking about biochemical weapons."

He was quiet for a moment. Then, "My gut is inclined to agree. I'll see if we can steal a march on them. Meanwhile, can you see a way to execute the mission?"

"I'm working on it."

"All right. Don't think too long."

"Ten four."

I hung up and sat looking back up the road. Working on it. I turned the words over in my head. I had exactly no idea how I was going to execute the job. But I wasn't about to tell the brigadier that.

I stood and started walking back toward my hotel. As I walked, I pulled up the other number the brigadier had given me on that phone. It was answered on the second ring. The voice sounded like it had been steeped overnight in a solution of whiskey and nicotine. It just said, "Yeah."

"Is this the Expatriate Ladies for the Protection of Cats Association?"

It was something the brigadier had come up with, born of his love of Cold War espionage novels.

"You Harry?"

"I need to know—"

"Yeah, yeah, we rescue three hundred homeless kitties each month. We're on a secure line only you and me have, pal. Who the fuck is going to be listening in? I'm CD. You're Harry, right?"

"What if I was Bob?"

He laughed unexpectedly. "Then I'd invite you over for whiskey and I'd gut you. You want some hardware?"

"Yup."

"Ponggol Seventeenth Avenue, by the Marina Country Club." He gave me a number. "It's a nice place with a dirty fence and a lot of palm trees. Call me when you're here and I'll let you in. Where are you?"

"Downtown, national library."

"I'll expect you in an hour."

"I'll be there."

I hung up and sat wondering for a while if choosing hardware would give me some idea of how I was going to use it.

TEN

I STROLLED BACK TO THE HOTEL, RODE THE ELEVATOR to my suite, removed my wig and beard, had a shower, changed my clothes, and told reception to bring around my Maserati.

Singapore is tropical, and the temperature is always between a low of about seventy and a high between ninety and a hundred degrees. The humidity is high, and that does not make for a comfortable environment. It makes you thirsty, but the more you drink, the more you sweat, and the more you sweat, the thirstier you get.

The heat had been building through the morning, despite the relatively cool breeze coming off the strait to the south of the island. It was the kind of weather that makes you hanker after a Mustang convertible or an AC Cobra. Unfortunately, the Maserati had no soft top, so I switched on the AC, pulled out onto Hill Street, and headed north and east toward Punggol.

I cruised at a steady, easy pace through prosperous suburbs of what felt like a middle-class Eden. You couldn't help feeling that here, even Elohim and Lucifer would both be members of the country club, Adam would have a good SUV and a power launch for fishing on the weekends, and Eve would have her own career and a therapist she couldn't afford not to have. It was like a utopia some dark bitter side of me wanted to prove was a dystopia, but as I drove past the pretty houses with their front and back yards overflowing with abundant palms and exotic flowers, I knew the statistics were against me. Somehow these people made it work.

Maybe, unlike us, the West, they had actually learned something from the Age of Empire and two world wars.

After three quarters of an hour or so, I crossed over the Tampines Expressway and descended along Punggol Way into Punggol itself, an area which reeked of prosperity and success, cleanliness, order, and stability. Another five minutes driving beside the elevated metro brought me to a turn-off for what looked like a very exclusive residential area. Gunrunning was obviously profitable in Paradise. Maybe CD was selling to the Fallen Angels.

I found Seventeenth Avenue, followed it around in a stunted S, and came to the house he had described. I called his number again. He didn't answer, but his gate swung open. I nosed in and followed the drive around to the back of the house, where he had a large lawn surrounded by abundant trees and a gravel parking lot beside a long terrace. The terrace was contained within a wooden structure over which an abundant vine had swarmed, hanging down over the sides and casting the terrace into deep shade.

CD was standing by the entrance to the terrace with his hands shoved in his pockets and his shoulders slightly hunched. He was in a military sage sweatshirt and jeans. His hair was thinning on top, but he had a long ponytail and a dark goatee. I figured he was in his forties, scrawny and hard—and dangerous.

I climbed out of the Maserati, and as I stepped toward him, he pulled out a cell phone and took a picture of me. He spoke like a spade going through gravel while he sent the picture.

"I sure hope you're Harry. I'd hate to have to kill you. You look like a tough customer."

"Neither of us is dead yet. I guess that means something."

"Sure does." He nodded once at the screen and put his cell in his back pocket. "FR back at HQ says you're okay. That's good enough for CD." He held out his hand. "Good to meet you, Harry. Come on in and have a beer."

We shook, and I followed him through to his covered terrace. There was a wrought iron table with a couple of chairs. Beside them was a red fridge. He pointed to a chair, and I sat. He pulled out a couple of beers, popped them, and handed me one. He raised his and pulled off half before sighing and wiping his mouth with the back of his hand.

"Always thirsty in this goddamn place." I gave my head a twitch, and he studied me a moment. "You want some hardware. What are you looking for, a derringer, a 416, an armored vehicle...?"

It was a good question. The brigadier had said this guy could be trusted and would provide whatever help I needed.

"Maybe you can recommend something. I have a hit in town, staying at Raffles. We are out of time, and we have done no recon."

He laughed. It was more like a cough, but he was laughing, and I didn't blame him. He reached in his jeans and pulled out a paper pack of unfiltered cigarettes. He poked one into his mouth and lit up with an old brass Zippo.

"What the hell," he said with smoke puffing out on his words. "It happens. You do a hundred jobs where you trained for every goddamn detail that could go wrong. Then you get that job where everything goes wrong and they didn't train you for a goddamn thing. And that's where all that training actually becomes useful. Right?"

I nodded. "Right."

He raised an eyebrow. "Hit was somewhere else and target got away?"

"Yup."

He sucked on his cigarette, then dragged air in through his teeth. "And you're on a deadline, but you don't know what his routine is."

"Right, only it's not a he, it's a she."

He went very still, staring at the tabletop. When he spoke, his voice was very quiet.

"We don't kill women or children. Buddy don't kill women or children."

"That's why I told you. Anniken Larsen. Heir to the Nick Galkin arms shipping empire."

"Galkin's dead?"

"Yeah, you know him?"

"I buy and sell arms, man. Of course I know him."

I gave a single nod. "I killed him a week ago in New York. My targets were Galkin and his personal assistant, Anniken Larsen, whom we had assumed was a man. Turned out she was a woman. Right now, the intelligence we have is that she is shipping biochemical weapons to Russia, probably for use in Eastern Europe."

"Shit, man."

"They had a set-up. They identified countries with trade embargos against them. Say the sanctions against some Middle Eastern country that finances terrorism means it can't sell oil to the European Union. But the Pacific Island of King George is free to trade with both Europe and Iran. So Nick registers a trading company in King George and has that company buy crude oil from Iran."

CD took a pull on his beer and sighed as he set it down. "He still can't sell it to Europe because it has Iranian provenance."

I nodded. "But what he can do is sell it to another trading corporation, also belonging to him, which is registered in Indonesia. The cargo is transferred to another ship, where the bill of lading shows the petroleum was bought in Indonesia. It no longer has Iranian provenance. From there, through perhaps another couple of buyers and sellers, all belonging to Nick Galkin, the goods arrive in Europe after a short delay, at a considerably higher price."

He shrugged. "I'm not feeling my blood boil, Harry. It's bad.

Iran finances terrorism and should be stopped. But it's not grounds for killing a woman. We don't kill women and children. Period."

I watched him a minute, wondering if I was going to have a problem. I picked up the beer and drank. As I set it down, I told him, "I had a meeting with Galkin, one of his accountants, and Anniken Larsen about a week ago. I was buying cutting-edge military technology. I led them to understand my principal was Russia and that we were going to deploy those weapons against Eastern Europe. They told me they could get just about anything I wanted short of the Northrop B-2. They also told me that the source of most of their high-tech weapons systems was a branch of the Rat Labs in Sinaloa."

"You're shitting me."

"You can confirm all this through the brigadier."

"It's still—"

"How about if I tell you that I overheard a conversation this morning between Anniken Larsen and two Russians in which the Russians were kicking up a fuss because they hadn't received their cargo? What if I told you that cargo originated in the Sinaloa Rat Labs, and the CIA, the brigadier, and I are all convinced it is a biochemical weapon intended for use against Ukraine, Poland, Finland..."

I trailed off and reached for my beer. Before drinking, I said, "I'll tell you something else, CD. Even before I knew who she was, even when I was talking to Galkin, I had the feeling the person I was really talking to was her. That woman, along with that whole organization, is responsible for the slaughter of more women and children than we can count. She is a parasite who feeds off war and indiscriminate slaughter. She is no more a woman than Putin or Mohammed Deif are human beings."

He turned a grunt into a sigh. I pressed him.

"In New York, I managed to damage the network of companies and bank accounts that allowed them to carry out their trade, and I killed Galkin and his right-hand man, but if she is not stopped, she will rebuild it, and we will see indiscriminate slaughter spreading from Israel to Finland." I leaned forward and put my elbows on the table. "CD, the Second World War wiped out some eighty million people, and all that killing hinged on an axis of three regimes: Germany, Italy, and Japan, that were driven by two obsessions: political and military supremacy and, in Germany's case, the extermination of the Jewish people. Today we have the same dynamic, but now it's Russia, China, and Iran. All three are obsessed with political and military supremacy, but in Iran's case, they are also obsessed with the extermination of the Jewish people. We have seen the lengths they are prepared to go, and Anniken Larsen is one of those helping to arm this axis of evil with weapons of mass destruction designed by the Western military industrial complex. She has to be neutralized."

Something told me I'd said enough, and we sat in silence. I drank my beer, and he stared at the tabletop. Eventually he took a deep breath.

"I don't need a history lesson, Harry. I've been there, I've seen it and done it and got the wet T-shirt. I know women can be as bad as men, and so can twelve-year-old kids if you teach them right. And what we're about is taking out the trash, right? Whether the trash is a man or a woman. I get it, but I don't have to like it."

His cigarette had burned down. He pulled over a metal lid from a jar that had three butts stubbed out in it and stubbed out the fourth. As he spoke, he pulled another cigarette from his pack and lit it with his Zippo.

"So either you take her out at the hotel or just outside it, or you lure her to a location of your choice."

"Right. I took Galkin out at the hotel, in my suite, so she is going to be on her guard. Plus she knows me."

"Okay, so a sniper shot from a surrounding building, a bomb or lure her to some place of your choice." I drew breath, but he raised his hand with the cigarette trailing smoke between his fingers. "The sniper shot raises problems of extraction; it also has a high risk of collateral damage, as does the bomb. The bomb also requires time and surveillance to establish where and when you plant it. Which leaves you with luring her into a trap."

I nodded. "Agreed. And that would open up the type of weapon that could be used." I paused a moment, and we both spoke at almost the same time. "The Russians."

He nodded. "Right. You need to take out the Russians. But before you do that, you use them to arrange a meeting, somewhere remote. When she gets there, bang. Bomb, sniper, M 134 minigun, whatever you want."

"It's good. I'm a tourist here. You know the place. Any suggestions for a location?"

He eyed me a moment. "Yeah, I got a pal who has a warehouse out by Tuyas. Let me talk to him. I'll call you this evening. Meantime you need to get a hold of those Russian guys. How are you going to do that?"

I sighed. "Yeah, options are a thing I'm pretty short on. Tail, observe, make a plan and execute it would be nice, but it also requires time. And time is something I haven't got."

"So you approach them." He grunted, sighed, and looked away, like he'd spoken without his own permission. "I shouldn't get involved," he said. I was going to tell him nobody was asking him to, but he cut me off. "Singapore isn't Malaysia. That's anarchy up there. You can do what the hell you like, and a few bribes will get you off the hook. Here it's different. We have to be careful."

"CD, I am not asking you to get involved."

"Yeah, I know that. But you're going to need a wingman. You can't do it alone."

"What the hell are you talking about?"

He shook his head, blowing smoke through his nose. "Don't get sore, pal. I know you're good. Buddy says you're the best, and if he says that, it's true. But like I said, this ain't Malaysia. You can't just pull up and bundle two guys in your trunk. Within ten minutes, you'll have twenty guys calling the police, all of them having made a note of your license plates and the make, model, and year of your vehicle. Not to mention what you were wearing." He pointed at me, squinting through the smoke. "And don't try and bribe the cops. They'll just add ten years to your sentence. You need a wingman, somebody who knows the place and how it works." He shook his head. "God dammit!"

"What are you telling me, CD?"

"I'll tell you what, Harry. Have some lunch. See if you can get a location on these bozos. I'll talk to my pal about the warehouse, and I'll have a think. You're right. I know the territory. I'll call you this evening and we'll have dinner." He grinned, then laughed like he was gargling gravel. "Don't worry. I clean up good."

He reached down beside him and came up with a leather bag which he slid across the table. He looked amused. I opened the bag and found a Sig Sauer P226, my weapon of choice. There was also a suppressor and a Fairbairn and Sykes fighting knife.

His smile had shifted to the right side of his face. "Buddy told me your preferences. He asked me to give you a hand if you needed it." I drew breath, but he raised two fingers holding the cigarette. "Not if you asked, pal. He said if you needed it. You need it, believe me. I'll call you this evening. We'll eat."

I thought about it, then nodded. "Thanks." I showed him the weapons and made a question with my face. He said, "Taken care of."

I stood. "I'll be waiting for your call."

I got in my car and headed back into town.

ELEVEN

I TOOK A ROUNDABOUT ROUTE AND ENDED UP AT THE Jumbo Seafood East Coast Restaurant, which was actually on the south coast, overlooking the Singapore Strait. Clouds had gathered above, and the water was more gray than blue and bristled with lots of angry little waves.

The restaurant had a huge terrace that was bustling with noisy families gorging on crabs and prawns and fish. They all seemed to have their fingers stuck out, covered in fishy sauce, or were licking them and wiping them on paper napkins. I gave the place a miss and found a small park with what looked to me like jacaranda trees. There I found a place to sit where I could look out over the water at the mass of tankers that sat bobbing on the restless water.

I called the brigadier.

"Harry, you're calling too often."

"I know. It's not the only thing that's wrong. Your man CD is recruiting himself on to the job."

"Let him. He's a good man. He's been there a long time, and he knows the ropes. Singapore is not like the rest of Southeast Asia—"

"Yeah, he told me. He also told me you'd instructed him to help me if I needed it. Not if I asked for it, if I needed it."

"That is correct."

"You could have told me, sir."

"How would you have reacted?" Instead of answering, I sighed. "He's been with us for years, Harry. He can be very useful. Are you done complaining?"

"Yeah."

"I made some calls. MI6 told me they were aware of the arrival of Vlad and Ivan in Singapore and were watching them. They are Vladimir Sokolov and Ivan Vasiliev. They are being monitored by the Five Eyes, and ODIN confirmed this."

"You're on speaking terms with the Norse gods?"

"It's an intelligence department, Harry. They tell me Sokolov and Vasiliev are staying at a Russian safe house on Jin Pisang, just off Victoria Street. Number 9B. It's apparently a small apartment above a café. I am guessing you will use them to get to Larsen."

"Is that you telling me this, sir, or CD?"

"Me. I haven't spoken to him yet. When I do, I will make him understand you are in charge of this operation. But trust him, Harry. His knowledge of the area will be valuable to you."

"Yes, sir."

I hung up and sat thinking for a short while. Then I called CD again.

"Hey. That's a lot of calls, pal."

"Yeah. Listen, I heard the guys are in town. I'm going to drop in and say hi. I thought we could go to a party after."

"Cool. Say three a.m."

"Right."

I hung up and walked back to my car.

I didn't drive back into town. Instead I turned east and made my way back to the airport. There I left the Maserati in the parking lot and rented a generic car that might have been a Honda or a Nissan, a Volks-Audi or a Peu-Citroen Benz. I didn't know or care. What I wanted was its generic style and total lack of character.

From the airport, I drove it the twelve miles to town, pulled into Northbridge Road, and then nosed into Jin Pasang.

Jin Pasang was a short alleyway lined with cafés and small shops. I had to spend a half hour going around in circles but finally found a parking space and settled to watch number 9.

Dusk was closing in by the time they showed up. They did it with all the style and subtlety that makes the Russians stand out from everybody else. They pulled up in a chauffeur-driven Mercedes sedan with diplomatic plates. They climbed out, went in through a door beside the café, and disappeared from view.

I climbed out of my anonymobile and strolled up to the door, pausing to look in a couple of shop windows on the way. The door beside the café said 9B in brass letters. It stood ajar, and I pushed inside. There was a narrow passage and then a single flight of stairs to a small landing and a door. I fit the suppressor to the Sig as I climbed the stairs.

I rang at the bell and waited fifteen seconds. Then an ugly voice growled through the door, "Who?"

I forced a grin onto my face and said, "Oh, mistah, I from Yummy Takoyako restaurant downstair. You friend bring parcel for you. Leave with me. I bring."

I was pretty sure I had guaranteed myself a special place in Woke Hell, but it seemed to have worked. There was a long silence, maybe twenty seconds, then I heard the latch click, and the door opened.

I didn't wait for him to get it all the way open. I made a rough guess and triple-tapped him in the head through the door. I put my weight against it and heaved and heard him hit the floor as I slipped through.

Directly opposite me, there was a bathroom. The door was open, and the light was off. The guy I recognized as Ivan with the sandy hair was lying slumped across the door. His face looked like somebody had sat on a bunch of tomatoes, and what brains he'd had were all on the wall and the coats hanging from a rack by the bathroom door.

To my right there was only a wall. To my left there was an open door that gave onto what looked like a living room. There was the sound of a TV, then a voice, deep, rumbling. It said, "Ivan...?"

I took two strides toward the door and caught him as he was coming out, frowning. I said, "*Freeze!*" but this guy was seasoned and good. He didn't even look surprised. He grabbed the barrel with his left hand, smashed his right into my wrist, and levered the weapon back, aiming at my chest. Another second and I'd have been joining Ivan at harp practice in hell.

I turned savagely to my right and stamped viciously at his knee. He took the pain and kept levering the Sig, like he wanted to break my wrist and my fingers. We stumbled back against the wall and the coat rack. The wall gave me support, and I rammed three savage kicks at his lower belly with my left foot. The first two scraped off his thigh, but the third connected and sent him staggering against the doorframe.

He didn't stay there long. I was leveling the Sig at his leg, trying to ignore the pain in my wrist, but he was already bouncing back, snarling through his twisted face. I fired, the weapon kicked, but the slug missed him and thudded into the wall. Then he had my wrist in both hands, forcing it up at the ceiling and lashing out at my knee with his right foot. I kept moving, circling to my right, trying to keep my knee out of range.

He lashed out twice, and on the third, I timed it so that as his foot left the floor, I moved in and rammed my instep into his balls. His face contracted, and his eyes were suddenly rich with pain and fear. He knew he was going to die. He gripped hard on to my right hand, where I still held the Sig, as his face twisted with the debilitating pain.

I didn't telegraph it. I drove my left fist hard into his chin. It was like punching concrete, but he staggered, his pupils dilated, and he let go of my hand. I used it to pistol-whip him, then kicked him in the chest and sent him crashing backward through the door into the living room.

He was semi-unconscious, groaning and trying to focus his eyes. I took one of his shoelaces and tied his ankles together real tight. I used the other to tie his right wrist to the belt loop at the back of his pants. Then I went to the kitchenette, filled a glass with water, brought it back, and threw it in his face. He gasped, coughed and spluttered, then stared at me.

He said, "Who...?" but it was like he had too many questions crowding his mouth and he couldn't finish.

I said, "You speak English. I know you speak English. So I am going to ask you some questions. You are going to answer me. If you don't, I am going to get a pair of kitchen scissors and cut your fingers off. First the pinky, then the ring finger, then the middle..." I paused. "You understand me. Now my first question is this: Do I need to prove to you that I am serious?"

He didn't answer. He stared at me. His pupils, which had been huge, were now pinpricks. Beads of sweat were popping out on his face. I stood and walked back into the kitchen. I opened the cutlery drawer noisily, pulled out the kitchen scissors, and slammed it closed again.

By the time I got back to him, he was struggling to get into a sitting position and beginning to whimper. I put the muzzle of the Sig on his lower belly, and he went very still. I showed him the scissors.

"Do I need to convince you that I am serious?"

He swallowed hard. "No."

I nodded. "Good. Why are you here in Singapore?"

"Work at embassy..."

I gave no warning. I hammered the butt of the Sig hard down on his hand. He yelped with the pain. I grabbed his pinky, twisted hard, and pulled his arm out straight. I put my right knee on his wrist, shoved his pinky between the blades of the scissors, and heaved all my weight on them. I felt the cartilage crunch, and the finger dropped off.

His scream was appalling. His eyes rolled up, and he groaned, slipping into unconsciousness. I returned to the kitchen, found some twine in a bottom drawer, returned, and cut a piece a foot long, which I tied tightly around the stump to stop the bleeding. A saucepan of water brought him around.

He blinked away the water and stared at me, his lower lip trembling and curling in.

"Vladimir Sokolov," I said. He frowned. "It was a trick question. I already knew the answer. Now we are going to try again. This time you will know I am serious. Next time you lie or hesitate too long, it's your ring finger, then the middle." I shrugged. "Then we go direct to the wrist. Why waste time, right? You understand I am serious, and you need to be asking yourself, is it worth it? Keep lying to me, Vladimir, and you will end up dead. Not soon, but you will die. On the other hand, be cooperative, be helpful, and you might end up with a nice house in California, supplying the CIA with useful information. You have to make a smart choice, right?"

He nodded. I smiled. "So tell me, why are you in Singapore?"

"We have to make contact with agent of arms dealer. We make order, and it is not delivered. We want to know where is."

"Good. Did you talk to the director of the company?"

"No. He is not available."

"Who did you talk to?"

"His assistant."

"Name?"

His lips worked, he was struggling to remember. "Norwegian woman, good-looking, name like Star Wars, Darth Vadar before he is with the dark force, Anniken! Anniken Larsen!" He laughed and cried at the same time, staring into my face. I felt nauseated and fought the urge to feel compassion.

"Where is she?"

"Raffles Hotel."

"What did she tell you?"

"She is looking for, maybe in Bay of Bengal, Africa..."

"The product."

"Eh...?"

"You called it the product."

"Yes." He was disorientated. His eyes showed terror. "The product..."

"What is the product?"

"Is biochemical product."

"A weapon?"

"Yes, weapon."

"A new weapon?"

He started sobbing and shaking his head. "Please, I don't know. Is new I think, WMD, weapon of mass destruction. I think. But we don't know. We just have to make pressure on agent. Please, believe."

"Relax. I believe you."

I reached in his pocket and pulled out his cell. I showed it to him.

"You are going to call her. You are going to tell her your section chief has arrived from Moscow and wants a meeting with her. He wants to know if their network is still functioning, and he wants to extend the order and introduce her to an Iranian client who is looking for weapons grade plutonium. You understand?"

"Yes, CIA. You CIA, yeah?"

I made him repeat it several times till he had it. Then I told him, "You tell her to go to this address. Boris will be waiting there with you. You tell her Ivan has been sent back to Moscow."

I pulled him into a sitting position, propped him against a chair, gave him the cell, and put the Sig in his face. "Do it."

"If I do, CIA..."

"You get a free ride to Los Angeles courtesy of Uncle Sam. Stop calling me CIA."

He nodded a few times, then dialed. It rang a couple of times, then her familiar voice came on the line.

"Yes?"

"Ms. Larsen, this is Vladimir Sokolov."

"I have not had time yet to—"

"That is not the purpose of my call. I am quite sure you are doing everything you can. I been talking with my head of section. He asks me my opinion."

"Your opinion of what?"

"If I think you will find product. I tell him I am sure. I tell him Nicholas will not try to trick us, and you are his most trusted partner."

There was a silence. "So...?"

"So he has more business for you. Ivan was insolent to you. I tell my boss, and he is go back to Moscow. He will no bother you again. Anniken, Ms. Larsen, we have urgent need, but very few suppliers like Nicholas Galkin. We need your cooperation. He has special order for you, and he want introduce you to Iranian, new client who has important order." He paused, glanced at me. I gave him a nod. He was doing okay. He said into the phone, "You can get plutonium? Weapons grade plutonium?"

She was quiet so long I began to think I'd overplayed my hand. Vlad and I stared at each other in silence. He was sweating profusely and had turned the color of candle wax.

Then she said, "Yes, I can get weapons grade plutonium. How much does he need? How soon?"

"He will tell you. I make only arrangement for meeting."

"Where? At what time?"

"Have to be very discreet. 26B Tuas Crescent, on the corner. There will be only my section chief, Iranian client, and driver. You will come alone with your driver."

"What time?"

"Three o'clock this morning. And, Ms. Larsen, my chief has tell me to inform you, Iranians are desperate. You can name your price."

There was just the hint of a smile in her voice. "And charge your boss less, right? Okay, I hear you."

She hung up.

He stared at me. For a few seconds, there was hope in his eyes. "I do okay, eh? CIA? I do okay..." But the hope faded, replaced by weeping misery. He knew. You always know. It's like some part of your mind can read it in the air. His head flopped to one side. “Come on, CIA! I done okay. I help...”

I took the phone from him and put it in my jacket pocket. Then I put a round through his forehead.

In my book, you don’t get to negotiate the purchase of a biochemical weapon that is going to kill soldiers, men, women, and children as well as babies, the aged and the infirm, and then feel sorry for yourself and get off scot-free.

I scrounged around the apartment for a while. I didn’t find much aside from a couple of tablets and Ivan’s cell. I didn’t figure they’d be much use, but I took them and made my way back to the car.

I drove back to the airport and switched back to the Maserati, which I drove to my hotel and arrived just in time for a shower and a change of clothes. It was as I was pulling on my jacket that I heard the knock at the door.

TWELVE

There was a guy in a well-cut blue suit. He was Chinese, tall and elegant. He smiled at me and spoke in the kind of cut-glass English you'd normally associate with Hugh Grant.

"Mr. Bauer?"

"Who are you?"

"Inspector Michael Lee."

"Is that supposed to mean something to me?"

He reached in his pocket and pulled out a wallet with a badge. It had a picture of him on it and said he was an inspector with the Singapore Police Force. I handed it back.

"What can I do for you?"

He raised an eyebrow. "Well, you could let me step inside for five minutes so we don't have to talk out in the corridor."

I stepped back, and he came in. I pointed to the sofa. "Can I offer you a drink?"

"No, thank you, Mr. Bauer, not while I'm on duty. I won't take up much of your time." He sat, and I sat in the armchair across from him. "As I am sure you know, the British have very close ties with Singapore in the areas of defense, antiterrorism, and intelligence gathering."

"Sure."

"So they would like to know, Mr. Bauer, what you are doing in Singapore."

"Why?"

He smiled. "Do we have to play games?"

"I don't know about you, Mr. Lee. I'm not playing any games. As far as I am aware, I don't need a special reason to visit Singapore. And why I am here is none of their damn business, or yours, for that matter."

He was unfazed. "Well, that's what I am here to find out, Mr. Bauer. Whether your visit to Singapore is, in fact, any of our or their damn business. The British SIS informs me that they are aware of you. They are aware that you work for the United States government, and I am asking you in the least offensive terms I know how, why are you here?"

I watched him for a long count of five. Then I leaned forward. "If you know that much, Mr. Lee, then tell the British Special Intelligence Service to go ask my boss why I am here. But I'll tell you what I think. I think, if you haven't done that already, it's because you don't know shit. You're fishing, and I'm not sure I believe you're even a cop. Last time I checked, the SPF were pretty good professionals. So why don't you take that piece of plastic you got from your box of cornflakes this morning and get the hell out of my room?"

I stood, and he stood too. "I'm sorry you feel that way, Mr. Bauer. It does not seem to me to be a reasonable reaction. I will be compelled to look more closely at your case."

"I'm here on vacation, Lee, and as long as that vacation lasts, I don't want to see your face again. Get out."

He crossed the room with some loss of dignity and left.

I was debating whether to call the brigadier and have him talk to the British Secret Intelligence Service, otherwise known as MI6, when my cell rang. It was CD.

"Where are you?" It was like the sound of coarse sandpaper being dragged over petrified nicotine.

"Does it hurt?" I asked.

"What?"

"Your voice."

He laughed like he had a bad bronchial condition. "I once had a tumor in my throat. It died of nicotine and alcohol poisoning. Where are you?"

"On my way down to the bar in my hotel."

"I'll meet you there. Mine's a scotch, double, no rocks."

I went down and found the bar. I ordered a Macallan and a Bushmills and carried them to a table in the corner. CD showed up ten minutes later in a well-cut gray suit. He'd removed the stubble from his cheeks, but he still had the ponytail hanging down his back. He sloped across the room among the tables and sat opposite me.

"How ya doin'?" He took the scotch, raised it in a toast, and took a pull. "I spoke to Buddy. He says you're pissed because I'm trying to muscle in. No problem. You're in charge."

I didn't say anything. He leaned back in his chair.

"You were eight years in the SAS. You saw a lot of active duty. You know better than anybody what gets most soldiers killed, especially in special ops. Bad planning, right? Improvising is by definition not being prepared." He smiled, even made it look genuine. "I'm not muscling in, Harry. I was more than twenty years in the military. Most of that time I was in special operations. I seen a lot of good men die because they weren't prepared. I'm not here to cause problems. I'm here to help." He shifted his smile to the ironic side of his face. "Maybe you don't like my style. Maybe I'm not sensitive and inclusive. Hey"—he shrugged—"that's tough shit. Maybe I can fix you up with a cute counselor when we're done. Meantime, let's try not to get killed in the next forty-eight hours. Sound like a plan to you?"

He drained his glass and signaled the waiter for a refill. I said, "You done?"

"I hope so. Are you?"

"Ivan and Vlad have taken early retirement." I took a sip of my Bushmills. "Ivan lost face and Vlad had a piercing headache."

"Not funny." But he chuckled anyway.

"They didn't think so either, but hey, that's tough shit, right?"

"Right."

"I can tell you that I persuaded Vlad to call a friend before he left."

"Yeah? Was she receptive?"

"Yup. She told him she'd always be there for him. At the appointed time and the appointed place."

The waiter brought over his drink. He took it and raised it in a toast. As he set it down on the table and smacked his lips, he said, "What do you say we have dinner and then go out to a club?"

I shrugged. "Sounds good to me."

We finished our drinks and went through to the dining room. There we ordered a couple of sirloin steaks and a bottle of claret. As he cut into his steak, he said, "You might want to think again about disposing of this client."

I stopped dead with my fork halfway to my mouth. Laid it back down on the plate and said, "What...?"

He chewed, watching me through narrowed eyes. He took his time, swallowed, and sipped some wine before answering.

"I've been nosing around, making some inquiries."

"Since when was that your brief, CD?"

"Brief? I ain't got no brief, Harry. Me and Buddy are pals. I lend him a hand sometimes. Nobody tells me what to do. You want to hear the rest or you want to go to the ladies' and straighten out your panties?"

He cut into the steak and put another chunk in his mouth.

"What kind of inquiries did you make?"

"I've been here a long time. I have a lot of friends here. I may have mentioned that. People trust me because they know I'm smart and I don't let my friends down."

"Yeah, I get it. That's moving. So what about—"

He cut across me. "You said they had a network of companies and shipping routes which you took care of."

"So?"

"So maybe you didn't take care of it completely. Word from the cops and a couple of friends at the British Embassy—"

"The British Embassy."

"Yeah, the British Embassy—word is Miss Larsen has been working her pretty butt off trying to rescue her inheritance from oblivion."

"Tell me something that isn't obvious. Surely that's the best reason we have to finish the job."

"Sure." He nodded. "Unless one of those companies was trading with Iran."

I scowled. "Iran?"

"What I am hearing on the grapevine is that her boyfriend's trade had picked up big time in the last three years, and all ears, electronic and flesh and blood, were listening hard to get some lowdown on who he was trading with. It was no surprise to find the chatter suggested Russia and Iran. China makes their own shit, but Russia is broke, and Iran needs to import all its goods. At one time, she could import shit from Russia, but the Five Eyes are watching what goes down between Russia and Iran like a hawk. You know Israel is like an honorary member of the Five Eyes, and if she gets the smallest whiff that Iran has a nuke, she will annihilate them. So Iran has to be real careful and do its shopping on the sly."

"So what are you saying?"

"I'm saying maybe you should talk to the lady before you take her to the dark place. Maybe you should hand her over to the Company at the US Embassy and let them deal with her."

I stared at him, remembering a day in Afghanistan when the CIA moved in on an operation we had executed and took a murdering bastard from our company so they could set him up in a pretty house in California to live out his days as a consultant to the CIA. I shook my head.

"That's not going to happen. She pays for what she's done."

He shrugged. "That's cool with me. I'm just saying, if she has merchandise that is already on its way to Tehran, NATO—not to mention the Mossad—should probably know about it."

I swore under my breath. "How reliable is your intelligence?"

"Very. It don't get much better."

"SIS?"

He sighed. "I can't reveal my—"

"*SIS?*"

"Yes, but don't ask me again. I don't work for you."

"Have you spoken to Buddy?"

He shook his head. "It's your show."

We finished our steaks in silence and ordered coffee. When it had been delivered, he said, "So what are we doing?" He glanced at his watch. "We need to make a move soon to set things up."

I nodded. "Right."

"We'll go in the Maserati. It'll be more convincing than my pickup."

I eyed him a moment and had trouble keeping the sarcasm from my voice. "Anything else?"

He raised his hands and shook his head. "Hey, we're two pals going out looking for chicks. You want to lighten up, Harry."

I gave a laugh and leaned forward with my elbows on the table. "Next time you tell me what I want to do, next time you give me a last-minute change of plan or call the brigadier behind my back, I am going to shove your night out looking for chicks right up your ass. I don't like last-minute changes to plans, and I don't like having the rug pulled from under my feet. Especially," I said, forcing another laugh, "when that puts control of the operation into somebody else's hands."

"Maybe we should talk in the car," he said, like he was chewing gravel. "If you smack me in the mouth in here, it might blow our cover."

"You have any more instructions for me, CD? I'm going to finish my coffee, and then we'll go and get my car. See if we can go and pick up some chicks."

I took my time finishing my coffee, then stood and led the

way out to reception. I had them bring the Maserati around and climbed behind the wheel. He climbed in beside me, and we headed down toward the West Coast Highway. As we crossed the Esplanade Bridge, I asked him, "How close are you to the British?"

He frowned at me, like he didn't understand the question. "Hey, I was with the Seals and Delta. You were the one who was eight years with the Regiment."

"Is that an answer?"

He sighed. "Man, you make this hard. I have been a long time in Singapore. The Brits run things here from behind the scene. I told you, anything military, antiterrorism and intelligence they run. So I am close to them."

"My question, CD, was how close?"

"I don't know what you're driving at, Bauer. The Brits are our allies. If anyone understands that, you should. Buddy is a Brit, remember? I'm not asking you how close you are with them. I'm close. We're allies. If you're questioning my loyalty to the US, you can stop the goddamn car and we'll discuss it by the damned roadside. What's your goddamn problem, Bauer?"

I didn't answer for a moment. Eventually I asked him, "You know a guy called Michael Lee?"

"No."

"He came to see me just before you called."

"So what?"

"He showed me an ID card which said he was an inspector with the SPF. He said MI6 wanted to know what I was doing in Singapore."

He looked out of the window at the passing sprawl of the port and the thousand lights of the ships moored out in the darkness of the ocean. "You're a smart guy, Harry," he told his reflection in the window. "So I am surprised you can't see how stupid what you're saying is." He turned to look at me. "I know why you're here. I know why you're here because Buddy told me. If I had told the SIS you were here, they wouldn't need to send some guy to find out *why* you were here. Because *I* would have told them already. Can you see that's stupid?"

I nodded slowly. "I can also see that from the moment I arrived here, you have been trying to take control of the operation. I can see that you have made enquiries with the British to which I was not privy. I can see that you have chosen the place and time of our meeting with Larsen. I can see a big mess and a lot of confusion which I don't understand, and I don't like it." I glanced at him. "The only reason we are in this car is because the brigadier has vouched for you."

The implication was clear, and he got it: The only thing standing between him and a 9 mm slug was the brigadier. He shook his head.

"I don't know what you want me to do. The Brits are not your enemy, that's for starters. In the second place, what I talked to them about was Larsen, not you. And in the third place, like Buddy already told you, I'm not taking control. I'm advising you in a territory you are not familiar with. And last of all, I have no idea who Michael Lee is or why he went to see you. Did you ask him?"

"He said MI6 knew about me, and they were watching me. They wanted to know why I was here."

He shrugged. "Maybe that's true. Like I said, if I was informing them, they wouldn't need to ask you. I would have told them you were here to hit Larsen. And after making inquiries back home, they'd probably have left you to it."

What he said made sense, but I couldn't shake a bad feeling that something was wrong. I was quiet for a while. He spoke suddenly as we passed the West Coast Park and the yacht club.

"Harry, if my life is at risk from you, I want out. Now I'm happy to risk my life in a worthy cause, fighting for Uncle Sam or in defense of Western Democracy. But I don't want to go down fighting for my life against a colleague who wants to kill me because he thinks I'm bossy. I also gotta tell you, if you take me out, you are going to have big problems with your brigadier. Me and Buddy are friends, and we go back a long way."

I sighed. "Relax. Your life is not at risk from me."

He watched me a moment. "Good." There was only a hint of humor in his rasp of a voice when he said, "I'd hate to have to explain to Buddy that I had to kill his best operative in order to save my own life."

I glanced at him and arched an eyebrow. "Point taken."

It was a point that hadn't been lost on me since I'd first met the guy. He played it down with his easy, laidback manner, but he was dangerous. This guy was about as dangerous as they get.

THIRTEEN

We arrived at the location at one a.m. To anyone accustomed to the desolation of Hunts Point in the Bronx or Wilmington in Los Angeles, or any industrial area of any Western city, Tuas would seem strange. It was clean and neat and well-kept, with plenty of street lighting and lots of trees and well-maintained grass shoulders. If you mugged someone here, you'd feel compelled to say please and thank you, maybe even apologize and return their purse.

We turned in off Pioneer Road onto Tuas Crescent. The streets were well-lit but empty, which made them oddly eerie. All the factories and warehouses were set back from the road among lawns, illuminated by spotlights, though the windows themselves were all dark.

After half a mile, the road bent to the right, but there was a small turn onto a driveway on the left. CD pointed to it and said, "Take the exit."

I pulled in and followed the drive. It made a dogleg and headed down toward the black water. Here there was less lighting, the blacktop gave way to a broad track of beaten earth, and the well-kept lawns were replaced with steel fences behind which all kinds of junk was strewn, from piles of old tires to broken motorcycles and stacks of wooden pallets.

A single-story building loomed suddenly on our right behind a line of tall palms. CD pointed at the gate and said, "This is it. Let's go in and prepare a reception party."

We climbed out. The doors echoed in the dim-lit emptiness. CD unlocked the padlock on the gate, and we pushed through and down the path to the main door. Here he produced another key and after a moment pushed the door open, and we went through into a large, dark space. The few, scattered rustles told me there were rats in the shadows. I heard a soft movement behind me, and the strip lights overhead flickered on.

The room was about a hundred feet long, left to right of where I stood. At the far end, maybe seventy feet away, there was a door in the wall that I figured led out to the wasteland outside. The far wall opposite where I stood was maybe fifteen or twenty feet away. The place practically empty but for odd bits of junk up against the walls. There was a table in the middle of the floor with a large kit bag on it and a large carton. CD closed the door and crossed the floor to the table. I followed, and he started opening the bag.

"You told her to come alone, like we discussed."

"Her and her driver. The chances of her following instructions like that are zero. She has no reason to."

"Agreed. You think she'll bring two or three SUVs, eight or ten men?"

I nodded. He pulled out eight cakes of C4 and handed them to me, then reached down beside the table and handed me four plastic cones with orange and white stripes.

"That's what I thought too. We can make a parking area for them. I'm the contact's driver—" He hesitated a moment. "What name did you give him?"

"Boris."

He smiled. "Okay, I am Boris' driver, and I will make sure only she and one man come in. They won't push it. She's hurting financially and needs the deal we're offering. She'll be suspicious, but when she sees only me and one car outside, she'll be happy to have her boys in the SUVs stay outside."

"You got it all worked out, huh?"

"I'm a good planner. You want to stuff the C4 into those cones, or am I being too controlling?"

I took off my jacket and started ramming the cones full of enough C4 to blow a fleet of SUVs to Mars.

"Okay, so you send the boys back to their trucks, and she comes in with her number one bodyguard. The minute she sees me, she's going to recognize me. We should have discussed this plan before—"

"Quit griping, Harry. There was no time. That was the first thing you told me. Besides, when she gets in here, she won't see anybody. Because you'll be outside, out that door at the end there."

He pointed to the door in the wall at the end of the hall.

"You'll be watching. When you see they are all safely in their vehicles, I close the door and you come in. You'll be wearing a heavy coat and a hat. You will not be recognizable."

I put the last of the cones on the table. "What hat and coat?"

He jerked his chin at the carton. "In there. I make like I am calling you. You come in. I press the detonator, and we shoot her guy. She'll be in shock, and I am pretty sure we can handle her. But I'd suggest giving her a dose of something to knock her out."

He reached in the back and pulled out two HK 416s and a large needle gun. He held it up.

"It's loaded with fentanyl and propofol. She'll go out like a light and sleep for an hour at least. It's up to you, man. But I think you need to talk to her."

I thought for a moment. "When that C4 goes off, we are going to have cops, firemen, and choppers swarming all over this area. How long are they going to take to get here?"

"Fifteen minutes, more than enough time to get her into the Maserati and get the hell out of here."

"Out of here, but where to? You keep moving the damn goalposts, CD! One thing is executing the mission and getting the hell out of here to a club or back to the hotel. But now we are loaded down with an unconscious woman. Where the hell do we go with her?"

He handed me an assault rifle, then opened the carton and shoved a coat and hat at me.

"Two miles northwest is the station. There is unimpeded access to wasteland there and the water. We have a seaplane waiting."

"*What?*"

"Don't start getting your panties in a twist again, Harry. You had a last-minute execution on your hands with no preparation and no goddamn extraction! I pulled strings and managed to get a hydroplane to get us out of here. Jesus, man! You're welcome!"

"Where the hell is it going to take us?"

He took a step toward me so we were barely inches apart. He was looking mad.

"If we quit wasting time, the Maserati can get us to the plane in less than three minutes, including loading and unloading time. We fly south, keeping low, for about fifty miles. Ten miles south of Sugi Island, we connect with a yacht."

"Are you out of your mind? Whose yacht?"

"Onboard there will be a captain and four hookers. If anyone asks, we spent the night partying with them. But nobody will ask. We keep going south toward Australia, and by the time we reach Bangka Island, we will have been picked up by the USS *Antietam*. You and Anniken will be airlifted back to the US, and I will be taken back to my home in Singapore."

I could feel hot anger and a twinge of fear burning in my gut. "When the hell were you planning to tell me all this? You arranged this whole damn thing since this morning? How fucking stupid do you think I am, CD? And who does this goddamn yacht belong to?" I shoved the Sig in his face and snarled, "You better start explaining, pal, and you better make it good!"

With my left hand, I pulled out my cell and dialed the brigadier. CD had raised his hands. He spoke quietly. "There's a jamming device under the pallets over by the door. I didn't want Anniken calling the Russian Embassy if things got complicated. Will you please relax? You already talked to Buddy, and he told you to trust me. I can answer your questions if you'll give me a chance."

"You better make it good, CD, because I am this close to blowing your goddamn head off."

"The yacht is a rental. I have a pal who rents out yachts. A lot of people rent yachts and sail over to Indonesian holiday islands. There is a big trade in cute hookers who get taken on those trips. The first thing I did this morning after you left was arrange the extraction, and that seemed to me to be a good option."

"What about this seaplane? You have a friend who runs them, too?"

"No. It's mine. I do a lot of trade with Myanmar, Malaysia, Cambodia, and Vietnam. The Singapore authorities turn a blind eye because I provide services for them, and"—he labored the words—"they are grateful. I am a useful guy. So the plane is mine."

"And I suppose the US Navy is also grateful to you, so you can call on a passing battle cruiser and have them pick you up when you're in the area."

"No, Harry. I haven't got that kind of leverage. But your pal the brigadier has. And no, I didn't arrange all of this since this morning. Most of it I did, but some of it was arranged by Buddy in the last week. Now will you please relax, put your damn gun away, and can we take the cones out to the parking area? We are running out of time."

There have been very few times in life when I have felt unable to make a decision. But in that moment I was paralyzed. I shoved the Sig in my waistband and took half the cones. He took the other half, and I followed him out to the silent street. As we started to set them out, he said, "When they arrive, I'll come out to guide them in among the cones. Meanwhile, you put on the coat and the hat and go out the back."

Back inside, he reached in the kitbag and pulled out a bunch of magazines for the HKs. He handed me three. "I can't imagine you'll need more than one, but better play it safe, right?"

I took them. Suddenly his face contracted with frustration. "Hey, Harry!"

"What?"

"I'm on your side, man!"

"I don't like the way you do things, CD. I don't like surprises, and I don't expect them from the guys I work with. Now I am going to ask you, is there anything else I need to know about this plan? Think hard before you answer. Are there any more surprises?"

He gave his head a single shake. "No."

"Right. You've told me no. The next surprise you spring on me I am going to blow you goddamn head off. Are we clear?"

"We're clear, Harry." He checked his watch. "They should be here in the next twenty minutes."

We made some last-minute arrangements, I killed the light over the far door from which I was going to enter, so that only the table and the main entrance were illuminated, and I stepped outside. CD stepped out to wait for the cars.

They arrived ten minutes later. As CD had predicted, there were two Range Rovers and one Audi Q7. CD stepped out onto the road, removed one of the cones, and signaled the cars where to park. They filed in, and after a moment, the headlights died. Then doors slammed, and I could hear voices murmuring. CDs was unmistakable, there were a couple of male voices and one female I recognized as Anniken. Then more doors slamming and steps approaching the warehouse.

Peering through the window, I saw Anniken, in jeans and a leather jacket, enter and pause, looking around. Behind her was a guy in a suit. Behind both of them was CD, standing in the open doorway. He looked in my direction, stepped inside, and closed the door. Anniken turned to speak to him. I opened the door and stepped inside. I was in shadow, with a large coat and a large hat. CD's gaze moved past Anniken to look at me. Anniken stopped talking and turned. We all stared at each other, and nothing happened.

FOURTEEN

To say nothing happened is not exactly accurate. Something happened. Anniken smiled.

"Hello, Mitch. It is Mitch, isn't it? Or..." She frowned and snapped her fingers, "What was it, CD? Oh, yes, Harry. Harry Bauer. I am told you have one hell of a reputation. But—" She made a face that said she wasn't impressed. "You walked right into this. You were really easy to catch. I thought a few times you were going to see right through CD, but you just kept doing what you were told and walked right into the trap. I can't say I am impressed, Harry."

I pulled the HK assault rifle to my shoulder and pulled the trigger. Again, nothing happened. I turned my eyes on CD. He was watching me with no particular expression.

I said, "You son of a bitch" and dropped the weapon on the floor. I threw the hat and the coat after it. If I was going to die, at least I wouldn't die looking like an asshole. I took a few steps toward Anniken and heard the door open behind me. Tramping feet told me six or seven guys had entered.

I said,

"How did you know I had traced you here?"

"I didn't. Your friend CD brought me the information. He has wanted me for a few years now, haven't you, darling?"

She asked it over her shoulder without taking her eyes off me. He glanced at her but didn't say anything. She took a couple of steps closer to me.

"There are only two things in this world more desirable or more valuable than a woman's body. Do you know what they are, Harry?"

"Take a hike."

"Violence and information. If you control those three things, you can rule the world."

"You going to kill me or torture me to death with cheap philosophy?"

"I haven't decided. I think I'd like to talk to you for a bit before I feed you to the sharks. CD?"

He came forward, and I saw he had the syringe gun in his hand. As he approached, I made up my mind I was going to kill him. My chances of getting Anniken now were in minus values, but I would at least take out that treacherous bastard. But as I tensed to move, a powerful arm locked around my neck and two more hooked around my elbows. CD looked me in the eye as he rammed the needle into my shoulder.

"Sorry, pal. This is what happens when you don't plan."

Then darkness closed in.

A LIGHT BREEZE touched my face. I could hear the soft lap of water. I had no memories, no recollections. Everything was just the gentle splish and splosh of the water and the soft touch of the cool breeze on my skin.

Then mud and grass smacked me in the face. A hard boot kicked me, and an ugly voice snarled, "Geddup! You think I carry you, asshole? Up!"

I opened my eyes, and the world was an ugly place. It was still dark, and I was lying face down in scrubby grass and reeds which were growing out of an inch of mud. I tried to get up and discovered my hands had been tied. Another kick and "Up, zasranets!"

There was activity all around me. I looked and saw Anniken and CD climbing into a dinghy. A couple of other guys were loading stuff into a second dinghy. I propped myself against the Range Rover I had been dragged out of and levered myself to my feet. The guy who'd woken me was standing in front of me, scowling, "Come on! Move! Move!"

"You're a regular Prince Charming."

I am pretty fast, especially when I haven't been drugged and kicked. But sometimes rage, hatred, and adrenaline can make up for that kind of drawback. I kicked him in the balls with my instep. It probably wasn't smart, but it was a damned good kick. His eyes bulged, and his jaw sagged. The pain and the astonishment froze him. One thing they teach you in the Regiment is seize every opportunity without hesitation, so I kicked him three more times in the same place. That was one genetic line that wasn't going any further.

I was treated to a shower of blows and kicks as I was shoved toward the dinghy where Anniken was sitting with CD. Behind me, I could hear groaning and voices arguing over the sounds of extreme pain. Then there was a crack, and the groaning stopped. They had no use for a cripple.

I was shoved into the boat, we were pushed out onto the water, one of the apes fired up the outboard, and we took off into the dark. The other boat was just behind us. Anniken and CD were sitting opposite, watching me. CD had what looked like a Glock 17 held loosely in his hand.

After a few moments, the great, dark hulk of what looked like a Canadair 215 amphibious plane began to emerge from the darkness. I had flown one—and crashed in one—before.[1]

They'd lowered a set of steps from a door in the fuselage behind the cockpit, and I was pushed and pulled up into the body of the plane. Inside, it was not what you might expect. The Canadair 215 amphibious plane is a workhorse. It's tough, adaptable, rugged, and it gets the job done. But what they'd done here was to panel the walls in pale beige and install a couple of leather sofas, a couple of highly polished walnut tables, and all the USB ports a millennial could dream of. It made me wince. It was like finding your favorite Irish wolfhound with pink bows in his hair.

CD caught my look and smiled. "Never trust a Russian with a point to prove."

"You a Russian with a point to prove, CD?"

He smiled on the ironic side of his face. "I'm just living the American dream, pal." He pointed at one of the high-polish tables. "Sit down. We need to talk."

I went and sat, with some difficulty, with my hands tied behind my back. "That's what every girlfriend I ever had told me before she shoved me under a bus."

"Yeah, big reveal," he said like he was gargling rocks. "Life sucks. Maybe you missed that day at school because you were out killing bad guys."

They finished clambering in. There were two pilots, two gorillas, Anniken, and CD, who'd sat opposite me. She sat at the table across the aisle with her seat half turned to face me.

"You are one major son of a bitch." She gave a small laugh. "I *really* want to hurt you." This time, her laugh was incredulous. "Do you have any idea how much trouble you have caused me?"

I frowned. "What do you think, Anniken?"

The door slammed closed, and after a moment, the engines roared into life. For the next couple of minutes, the noise made it impossible to talk. Then we were surging through a vast canyon of spray, the world fell away beneath us, and we were rising into blackness.

Once we'd reached cruising height and leveled off, I turned to Anniken again. "Why am I not dead?"

A small smile played across her lips. It should have been a pretty mouth, but there was something sick about it. "Because you are the rogue agent responsible for killing a dozen policemen with your booby-trapped traffic cones. And that dedicated professional Inspector Michael Lee will lead an investigation into your whereabouts that will probably lead to your eventual arrest. And if you are not killed while resisting arrest, you will no doubt be sentenced to hang. The death penalty is alive and well in Singapore and is carried out by what is known as long drop hanging. It's more humane than the standard form."

"I guess all the forensics have been taken care of."

"Of course."

"So where are we going? I figure we're not going to a party yacht full of hookers."

It was CD who answered. There was no humor in his face when he said, "Not exactly."

"What do you want from me?" I turned from CD to Anniken. "I'm alive because you want something. You could have killed me and left me at the warehouse and achieved the same end. If I'm alive it's because you want something from me."

This time it was Anniken who answered. "CD and I have a bet running. The prize is an important one. If he wins, he gets to screw me. You see, normally, Harry, I only hit the sack with men who weigh more than two hundred and fifty pounds and have the IQ of a confused gorilla. He is too smart and too skinny for my taste."

"You're boring me, Larsen. It's a simple question. What do you want from me?"

She shook her head, smiling, biting her lower lip, and exchanged a glance with CD. "I am going to hurt him so bad."

"Not yet. Don't blow it. The time will come, just hold on."

She looked back at me. "See, CD thinks you're CIA. He says he knows the CIA, and you have it written all over you. I say no. You don't get rogue operatives in Central Intelligence. Whatever crazy shit they might have done in the '60s, they are now a well-oiled machine. But you? You're a one-off. You're a crazy motherfucker who just wants to go out and kill people." She squinted and pointed at me. "I can see it in your eyes. You and me are soul mates, Harry. How much do you weigh? I might just give you a send-off."

I turned to CD. "Is this part of the torture? I have to listen to this shit?"

"Who do you work for, Harry?"

I narrowed my eyes at him. "Seriously?"

"We are on this plane, fourteen thousand feet above a very black, very empty ocean. As long as we are here, we are just talking. Exchanging views, maybe even negotiating. When we touch down, all that will change. When we touch down, the interrogation will be"—he smiled—"enhanced. We will enhance the interrogation in ways you never dreamed possible. You will weep and beg, and this lady here"—he pointed at Anniken—"will enjoy every moment of it. So my advice to you, Harry, is start sharing now before it's too late."

I gave Anniken the once-over and allowed myself a smile. "You won't enjoy it, Larsen, and I'll tell you why. Because long before you start your enhanced interrogation, I am going to tear your heart out with my bare hands and eat it."

She stood up, laughing without humor. "Son of a bitch!"

CD said, "Take it easy. Just answer the question, Harry. Make life easier for everybody. Are you CIA or not?"

"Negotiate."

"What?"

They were both looking at me with interest now. "You said we might even negotiate. But I have my hands tied behind my back. Psycho here has already told me she wants nothing more in life than to kill me slowly and painfully, and I trust you about as much as I trust a presidential candidate who thinks Palestine is on the South American continent. So I have a lot to offer you, but you have fuck-all to offer me. On the other hand, on the face of it, you can get everything you want from me while giving me nothing in return but a pain in my ass. Not ideal negotiating conditions, CD."

A smile spread slowly across his lips. "So you *are* CIA?" He glanced at her and grinned. "I promise to make it hurt, honey."

"I didn't say I was CIA, CD. I'm asking you how we negotiate. I'm a patriot, and I am tough, but even I have my limits, and I'm not crazy about the idea of Psycho here peeling my skin off and rolling me in salt. But if we're going to do some kind of deal, I need to know you'll do your part."

He looked at her. Her eyes were all over the place. She glanced from me to him again, then at the floor and then over at the cockpit while she chewed her lip. I sighed loudly and addressed CD.

"She's out of it. She's not even coherent. Who am I talking to here? Am I talking to you or am I talking to Estrogen Central over there?"

That hurt, like it was supposed to. She turned on me, and her eyes were bright, her cheeks were flushed right down to her neck, and she was mad.

"I should—"

I raised my voice to a shout. "Yeah, yeah! Maybe you should! Yadda yadda. You must be damned good in bed, sister, because I can't see any other damned reason why a guy as smart as Nick Galkin would have you by his side. You're hysterical, unreliable, overemotional, and about as smart as you are fat and ugly. You want me to treat you with respect, act like a smart adult." I turned to CD. "It's like talking to a fucking thirteen-year-old with her first period!"

"Enough!"

I was still shouting. "Cut the crap! What do you want? You want to torture and kill me or you want to negotiate? Make up your mind! Who am I talking to?"

She walked away and sat on the sofa. I held his eye.

"What can you tell us?"

"I can tell you whether they recovered a flying saucer at Roswell. You got any more stupid questions? I have access to a lot of highly classified intelligence. You know that."

"You share that intelligence with us and you go free. We give Lee a different body."

"We're wasting time, CD. There are two things I need to start me talking and providing proof for what I tell you. One is knowing that crazy bitch wants to kill me slowly and painfully. We have that. The second is proof that if I talk, you will hold up your end of the bargain."

"Okay, that makes sense. Just tell me one thing and then I'll give you your guarantee. Are you a CIA agent?"

I sighed. "There is no such thing as a CIA agent, CD. I am a CIA officer. Yes. So you get to screw the craziest bitch on the planet. Congratulations. Now my guarantees, please."

Anniken's voice came like a hiss. "Your guarantees?" She came and stood next to me. Her slim, flat belly was just inches from my face, and I felt the hard tip of a blade trail up my back. "Your guarantees," she said again. "How about I guarantee..."

"Don't do it." His voice came as a growl. "Not yet. If we don't make a deal with him, you can do what you like to the son of a bitch later."

It's not easy to look bored when someone has a stiletto placed over your fifth intercostal, but I managed it, showed my bored face to CD, and said, "Again, who am I talking to? You want to negotiate, I'll give you a lot more in a deal than I will if you cut it out of me. Also, if I give as part of a trade, you can confirm what I tell you. Torture me and you will never know if what I tell you is true or false until it's too late."

Suddenly her jaw went rigid and she hissed the words through her teeth. "I can make you talk! And you will beg to tell me the truth. *I fucking own you!*"

Her face flushed red, and the blade dug into my back.

FIFTEEN

THE BLADE DUG AN EIGHTH OF AN INCH INTO MY BACK, and she leaned in close to watch my face as she cut slowly across my shoulder blade. I bit so hard on my teeth I tasted blood, but I would be damned if I made a noise. When she was done, she showed me the tip of the blade. Her face was an inch from mine. She opened her mouth, stuck out her tongue, and licked off the blood. Then she put her lips to my ear and breathed, "You keep being a wiseass, Harry, and you will find out what pain really is."

I fought hard to keep my voice steady, but I was hurting badly. I looked at CD. "Are we done with this adolescent shit? Can the grownups talk now?"

"That's enough, Harry. And you, Anniken. There's more in play here than your egos. I don't know what guarantees you think I can give you."

"Let's start with you patch up my back, you untie me and give me back my weapon, and in exchange, I'll tell you about Iran."

She froze. I made like I was in too much pain to notice. I saw his eyes flick up to her, then back to me.

"What about Iran?"

"Fuck you."

"Patch him up." That was directed at Anniken. To me, he said, "You know I can't give you a weapon. But I'll untie you."

"What kind of goddamn guarantee is that?" I snarled.

"Come on, Harry! Don't push it. What have you got on Iran? If it's good, we can talk."

Anniken had left while we were talking. Now she came back with a bowl of water and a first aid kit. She untied me, took off my shirt, and started washing the wound with surprisingly gentle hands. As she spread antiseptic cream on it and applied closure strips, I snarled at CD, "You got something to drink in this shit hole?"

I heard Anniken's voice from behind me, as surprisingly quiet and gentle as her hands had been.

"I'll get it."

She went, and I heard the rattle of glasses and bottles. She returned with a bottle of Johnny Walker and three shot glasses. She sat next to CD and poured. I swapped glasses with her and knocked back the shot. She smiled, and they both drank. As she refilled, I started talking.

"Israel made it clear a long time ago if they ever believed that Iran was about to make a nuclear weapon, they would annihilate them. I believe that was the word the spokesman used at the time. Israel has between forty and eighty nuclear warheads and a wide range of delivery options, from bombers to intercontinental ballistic missiles. At fifteen thousand miles an hour, they can hit Tehran and wipe it off the map in four minutes or less."

They were quiet for a moment, then CD shrugged. "That's interesting, but it is not classified information."

"No, but what is is that the Company is convinced Nick Galkin was supplying Iran with essential hardware to make a nuke. Current and previous administrations seemed to think it was a good idea to turn a blind eye while Iran made bombs. Israel's warnings went unheeded by the administration, but not by the Pentagon or the CIA. We struck a deal with the Mossad.

We take out Galkin and close down his operation, and in exchange, they don't nuke Tehran."

CD rasped, "Shit..."

Anniken said, "So where does that leave us?"

"I'll tell you where it leaves you. With my department wondering A, where the hell I am and B, what the hell they tell the Mossad. I'll tell you a little more. The IDF will not wait. The moment they discover I have gone missing, they are not going to sit around contemplating their fucking navels and searching their souls. They are facing an existential threat, and they will strike preemptively."

Anniken shrugged. "So what do we care?"

CD glared at her like she was crazy. "We care because if Tehran ceases to exist, we don't get paid, dumbass!"

I sat forward and refilled my shot glass. I drained it and filled it again.

"Now you want the useful details, or are you just going to sit here and chew your nails?"

She said, "Details?"

"Yeah, sweetheart, where, when, how many, what happens before and what happens after. It's called intelligence. You should try some sometime."

CD growled, "Take it easy, Harry. Let's keep this friendly. So what are the details?"

"There are two of them, CD, fuck and you. You want the details, you give me back my Sig and my knife, and we talk about my security. And we talk about something else, too. We talk about how much Tehran is paying you and what my fucking cut is."

"*What?*"

While he gaped at me, she threw back her head and laughed out loud. I drained another shot and slammed the glass on the table. I looked at her and snarled. "That cut you gave me on my back is going to be expensive, sweetheart. And so is the intelligence I give you. Every secret I share is another nail in my coffin. And every nail in my coffin is going to cost you a few million bucks. So you choose, Anniken. Are you going to twist your panties and watch Tehran annihilated along with all your money, or are you going to open up to a new ally?"

The phrasing was deliberate, and I let my eyes tell her so.

She was smiling, and it was hard to miss the hint of admiration in her eyes.

"You are some son of a bitch. Half an hour ago you were a dead man. But you're not fighting for survival..." She turned to CD, who was looking uncomfortable. "He's not fighting for his life. He's fighting for control. He wants to come out of this a rich man."

I ignored her and turned to CD. "We're running out of time."

Before he could answer, I asked him, "Where are we going?"

Anniken answered, "Sri Lanka, a small town called Pottuvil on the east coast." She turned to CD. "Give him his gun and his knife. And let's talk business."

He swallowed hard, glancing from me back to her. "Now just hang on a minute."

"There's no time," I snarled. "I'm not moving in on you, CD. She's all yours! I don't give a damn about her! But if you want the intelligence I have, then I need security and I need money. And we need to sort this out *now!*"

Anniken narrowed her eyes at me. "The virus?"

I scowled at her. "*What?*" But I knew what she was driving at.

"The virus you used to bring down Nick's network."

I poured myself another shot and threw it back. The pain in my back was making it hard to think. "What about it?"

"I want it."

"You can't reverse—"

"I don't want to reverse shit, asshole!" Her eyes were bright, and her face was flushed again. "I want the virus."

I leaned back in my seat, staring at my glass as I turned it in my fingers, like I was working out how I could do that. After a while, I shook my head like I wasn't convinced.

"I don't know. It has to be designed for a specific target. The guy who made it belongs to a department which is practically impenetrable."

She came and hunkered down next to me, smiling up into my face. I was astonished to realize that she was not beautiful, but she was really, really pretty. She had the face of an angel, with delicate pink lips and beautiful blue eyes. A fallen angel.

The blade of her knife rested on my thigh, pointing where no blade should ever point. She smiled, showing very white teeth.

"You've noticed I'm crazy, right, Harry?"

"I've noticed your dad never taught you discipline."

Her mouth continued to smile, but her eyes looked like she was going to cry. CD covered his face with his hand. My hunch had been right, and I had found her exposed nerve.

"I switch. I've been told I have multiple personality disorder. I don't know what it is, but certain things spark me off, and I can get pretty wild."

I leaned toward her, feeling the tip of the blade pressing on my lower belly. "It's called being a spoiled brat. And it has a very simple cure."

The smile faded, and she spoke through gritted teeth. "I want that virus, Harry! Get me that virus and you and me can do crazy things together. We can get richer than Elon Fucking Musk! *I want that virus!*"

The blade pressed into my jeans. I acted fast. With my left hand, I grabbed a fistful of the hair at the back of her head and pulled, so her throat was exposed. Then I leaned over her so our faces were just inches apart. "I need," I snarled, "to think."

The guys with guns who'd been keeping in the background got to their feet. I ignored them. Slowly I grabbed the hand that was holding the knife and squeezed it. She gave a small gasp of pain and smiled. I didn't smile. I pulled the hand and bent her elbow until the blade was pressed against her own throat. I heard CD cock his weapon. He spoke quietly.

"Stop, Harry."

I ignored him too. It was like Anniken and I were the only people on the planet. I was looking hard into her blue eyes and fighting a growing desire to have her. "What have I got, Anniken? What have you left me? What have I got to live for? You think I give a goddamn if your drones blow my brains out? I swear if one of them twitches in a way I don't like, I will cut your throat and drink your blood before I'm dead."

I took the knife from her fingers. She let it go without resisting, and I rammed the blade into the tabletop. I still had her face an inch from mine. I growled quietly, "I need to eat, I need to sleep, and I need to think. But you get this in your head, Anniken: The next person who threatens me dies." I let go of her hair. "Get up and sit down."

She stood unsteadily. "You son of a bitch."

I ignored her and looked at CD, who still had his weapon in his hand. "Put that away, CD. I'm serious. The next person who threatens me dies. I don't want that to be you. What's in Sri Lanka?"

He looked at Anniken. She nodded. He said to me, "A shipment from Mexico. Biochemical weapons for Russia—"

"Ivan and Vlad's products?"

"Yeah, and components for nuclear warheads, including weapons grade plutonium."

I narrowed my eyes. My head was beginning to throb, and the pain in my back was eating away at my neurons.

"You're telling me an American lab is providing Iran with nuclear weapons to use against Israel? That doesn't make sense."

It was Anniken who answered. "An American lab in *Mexico*. You don't get it, Harry. You haven't understood yet, have you? You're CIA. Who does the CIA serve?" I watched her face. She was smiling again. "Do you serve the president? Do you serve the American people? Or do you serve some amorphous spirit called National Security? Who are your masters, Harry? The White House and the Capitol, or McDaniels Skyline, Anglo-American

Petrochemicals, Texas Global Chemicals, Nevada Delivery Systems..."

CD said, "Ike called it. He was right, the military industrial complex, now it's the military industrial intelligence complex. The CIA is a main part of that complex. You must know that."

Anniken said, "Who do you think is financing them? America has become a service provider, Harry. Israel has the banks, Iran has the oil, Mexico has the cartels, and between them, they finance the trillions of dollars that the complex needs to keep making weapons. So Rat Labs in Nevada makes weapons for America's allies, especially Israel. And Rat Labs Sinaloa, which doesn't exist, by the way, gets funded by other sources and makes specialist weapons for other markets. Nick was an important part of that process, Harry."

I studied Anniken for a moment. "So if the virus destroyed the network, how the hell are you going to prove ownership of the goods on the container ship?"

"I have a special relationship with the minister of trade commerce and food security. I spoke to him on the phone yesterday, and he is awaiting my arrival with bated breath."

"So he will release it and the shipment will go to Iran or Russia?"

"It goes to Iran, to Konorak, in the Gulf of Oman. They have a surprisingly large airport there. The biochemical agents will be flown to Russia, and the nuclear components will go to Iran."

I nodded. "Assuming Tehran still exists by then."

She became serious. "What are you going to do about that?"

"I don't know." I glanced at CD, wondering how much of a danger he was now. "I need some powerful painkillers and some sleep. When do we reach Sri Lanka?"

CD checked his watch. "In about five hours. Eleven a.m. local time, more or less."

"Give me some food. Let me sleep for four hours. When we get to Sri Lanka, I'll have a solution."

CD was watching me like he wanted to gut me and throw me into the Bay of Bengal.

"You better run it by me before you put it into action."

"I will," I said and wondered what the hell it was I was going to do when we got to Sri Lanka.

SIXTEEN

I SLEPT THE FULL FIVE HOURS AND WAS AWOKEN BY THE change in the sound of the engines and the jolt as we hit the water. Various pains that had been kept at bay while I slept—or at least woven in to my dreams so I didn't notice them—now grew teeth and claws and started biting into my back.

I swung my feet off the sofa where I'd been sleeping and bent to peer out of the portholes. We had slowed, and the wall of spray had dropped to a trail of foam beneath the wings. The ocean was very blue and blended almost seamlessly into an immaculate sky.

"Good morning." I turned. It was Anniken. She was standing in the narrow cockpit doorway, watching me. She was smiling. "How did you sleep?"

"Well enough. What time is it?"

"Eleven-fifteen. You'll sleep better tonight. We've booked the Kottukal Beach House. It's like a small colonial palace. You'll share my bed tonight. I'll heal your wound. It's the least I can do."

I grunted. "Is there any coffee in this crate?"

Her smile deepened. "I know your game, Harry. But I'll play it with you. It's a game I like. I'll get you some coffee."

I sat at the table, and as the engines stuttered to a halt and we rocked and swayed on the surf, I covered my eyes with my hands and tried to find something solid to hold on to. Everything was wrong and nothing was right. I heard the gorillas going about opening the hatch, dropping anchors, and lowering the dinghies. The smell of coffee reached me, and I felt her presence across the table.

I dropped my hands, and she poured me a cup of strong, black brew.

"You only know one side of me, Harry."

"Yeah? The side that would cut my throat if she got mad?"

"Be reasonable. Nick's empire was worth ten billion dollars and rising. You extinguished that in a few minutes. Last night, you were standing between me and..." She hesitated. Then, "I was going to recover some of that, and you were standing in the way. But if we were on the same side..." She let the words trail off. "I was with Nick for five years, and I never hurt him."

"You just screwed all his bodyguards."

She shrugged. "I like brutal men. Are you jealous?"

"Very."

She giggled. I sipped my coffee. Behind her, CD emerged from the cockpit. Anniken and I exchanged a look that was almost telepathic, that told me CD had to die. He said in his raw, gravel voice, "You slept. You any clearer as to what we do?"

I spoke into my cup. "You had coffee?"

"Four hours ago."

"I haven't. Have you got a four-inch gash on your back?"

"I thought you were a tough guy, SAS and all that shit."

"Let me have my coffee in peace, CD. Start taking the stuff ashore and setting up the house. Let me think."

He scowled at the back of Anniken's head. "You coming?"

She spoke to him while smiling at me. "You heard the man, CD. Get the place sorted while we have a think. And deal with customs, will you?"

He left noisily, slamming things.

She watched me finish my coffee, then said, "I'm going to

bathe you, put some clean clothes on you, and then we are going to have some lunch and talk. We have a lot to talk about."

I shrugged. "We can do that."

Hell, sometimes you have to take one for the team, right?

As it was, she confined herself to bathing me in a tin tub she got from the back of the plane in hot, soapy water with hands that were astonishingly gentle. I felt sick, twisted, and confused inside, and what had me most confused and sick was that the gentle way she bathed me and cleaned my wound—the wound she had inflicted—was soothing and therapeutic.

She dried me and dressed me, and we climbed down to the Zodiac that was moored to the steps. I fired up the outboard, and we sped away across the water toward the white sands of the shore, slapping over the small waves. Looking at her, sitting just a couple of feet from me, with her fine, platinum hair whipping across her face, it was hard to keep a grip on what I knew she was. She was a cruel, narcissistic sociopath who had no compunction about enabling and facilitating the deaths of thousands, even millions of men, women, and children. Yet she sat there, smiling at me with a goofy grin, her baby blue eyes, her Cupid's bow mouth, and skin that might have been eighteen years old as she fingered her fine hair from her face. It was wrong, it was messed up, and it was more than my brain could process right then. So I held her gaze and headed for the white sand of the beach.

She took me to a big shack of a restaurant at a place called the Chairman Beach and Children Park. We coasted in on the surf and hauled the dinghy up on the white sand. Then trudged barefoot the fifty yards to a long hut surrounded by palms. Among the trees, there was a playground for kids made of steel arches, roundabouts and climbing frames that had once, years earlier, been painted bright colors. Ruthless wear by children and the salt wind had long since faded them.

The place was crowded and noisy, but we found a table on the sand, not too close to the kids, and a smiling woman in flip-flops trudged over with a notepad and a pencil. Anniken ordered rice and curry and stressed she wanted it with meat, chicken, curried pineapple, grated coconut, potatoes, eggplant, and plenty of sambol. She also ordered two bottles of Three Coins Riva beer.

When the woman had gone, she sat back in her chair and watched me. We were sheltered from the wind and the noise of the surf, but her fine, platinum hair still crept across her face with the odd gust.

"So how do we do this, Harry? You must have noticed I have a big schoolgirl crush on you. I'm not hiding it. I'd like you to stick around. I think we could be good together."

I gave my head a small twist. "Yeah, we can have hours of fun in our own personal nuclear fallout shelter."

She giggled. "Come on, you know that won't happen. It's like the Cold War. Everyone is threatening, but nobody has the balls to follow through."

The smiling woman came over with the beers. I poured mine slowly into a glass while Anniken swigged from the bottle.

"I spent a lot of time in Iraq, Iran, Afghanistan, even Pakistan. I have also spent time in Israel. I can tell you one lesson I learned above and beyond all others."

"What's that?"

"Do not judge the Arabs or the Israelis by the same yardstick you use for everybody else. There is the world, and then there is the Middle East. If there is one mistake people make over and over, it's believing that people in the Middle East operate with the same pragmatism that we do. They don't. And the Israelis are probably the only people on Earth who understand that. Iran—Islam as a whole—really *does* want to annihilate Israel and the Jewish people. They really *do* want to convert, enslave, or kill all who do not convert. It's what their god told them to do, and they will do it. At any cost. Israel understands that, and they are prepared to act preemptively to avoid it happening and save their people and their country. Their survival depends on it. We could be looking at a nuclear strike on Iran within hours, days at most."

She shrugged. "Iran is big. Nobody goes there anyway. The fallout—forgive the pun—will be minimal."

"Yeah, sure, but remember, you don't get paid."

She sighed and rolled her eyes. "You gotta understand, Harry. I would be stupid to let you call your office. If I let you call in, how do I know you're not going to betray me? You could be stringing me along, selling me a crock of shit." She gave an incredulous laugh. "What, you're going to call in to Langley, 'Hey guys, I'm not dead. I've just gone over to the other side because they pay better. But hey! Don't worry. We're not really selling nukes to Iran.'"

"Obviously not."

"So?"

"What's the name of the ship?"

"You're kidding."

"Okay, so maybe you should tell me how you aim to get paid before Tehran gets wiped off the face of the Earth."

She looked skeptical. "Are you sure about that? I think you're just trying to scare us into letting you call home, like ET." She put on a stupid voice and stuck out her finger. "Harry Bauer call home."

She threw back her head and laughed, pulling her knees up to her chest. I waited till she'd stopped.

"All right, maybe you're right. But how likely is it that you are? And if you're wrong and I am telling the truth, what provision have you made to ensure you get paid before a preemptive Israeli strike? You are talking about a lot of money to gamble on a hunch."

She looked away at the sea. I pressed her.

"They are not going to pay you until they receive the goods, right?"

"They paid half." She scowled at me. "A half that has vanished into cyberspace, thanks to you."

"We'll come to that. So they pay the rest on delivery."

"Yes."

"Assuming you can get the shipment released in the next forty-eight hours, it will take three days to reach Konarak and another two or three days for the cargo to be checked and approved and Tehran notified. A week is the earliest you are going to get paid, and realistically, you are talking about two weeks or more."

I picked up my beer and took a long pull. As I wiped my mouth with the back of my hand, I told her, "Realistically, Anniken, you have to know that right now, as we are speaking, the Mossad and the IDF are having emergency talks. They know Galkin had components on their way to Iran. I was going to stop them. It seemed I had. Now I have disappeared... Draw your own conclusions. What would you do if you were the Israeli minister for defense? What would you do if you were Netanyahu?"

"So suggest something to me I wouldn't have to be stupid to agree to."

"Okay, let me talk to my Mossad contact. You and CD sit there with me. If I cross a line, you shoot me."

"What will you tell him?"

"I've had to go deep undercover. I've found the ship, and I have managed to get it detained in port. I am negotiating with the port authorities for them to allow US authorities to come and inspect it. I stress to him I need him to keep his mouth shut about me, who I am. I'm a source, nothing more, and inform the Mossad and the IDF that I am a 'reliable source.' I need at least a couple of weeks. After that, they can blow all hell out of Tehran for all I care. But I will need the name of the ship."

"I'll think about it." She paused and drew breath, but I cut her short.

"What the fuck are you doing with CD? Was he Galkin's choice?"

She giggled. "No, Nick didn't trust him. When you killed Nick and I ran back to Singapore, CD approached me. He had always liked me. We'd known each other in passing for a couple of years or three. He is so insolent, and he has that raw, gravel voice and he just came up to me and said"—she imitated his voice—"'You're in a mess, let me take care of things.'"

"Take care of things?"

"Salvage what could be salvaged from the mess you had caused and start to rebuild the empire."

"He was going to do that for you." She nodded. "Have you slept with him?"

The expression on her face was pure glee. "How is that any of your business?"

"Have you?"

Before she could answer, our food arrived. The smiling woman set it all out, told us to enjoy, and withdrew. Anniken started helping herself. I said, "Do you plan to answer the question or do I need to take you out into the palm trees and beat it out of you?"

"Take it easy, cowboy. I haven't slept with him, but he is always asking me. I guess I'll have to eventually. He won his bet, right?"

"No."

I started helping myself to rice and meat. She paused and narrowed her eyes at me. "You're not CIA?"

I answered without looking at her, with my eyes on the food.

"I am CIA. He did win the bet. You don't sleep with him, and he does not get to screw you." Now I looked at her. "Neither do your gorillas. The only guy who screws you from now on is me. And I want CD dead. By tomorrow. Any questions?"

"Now wait a minute, Harry." She was laughing, and her cheeks were pink.

"It's either you or him. The next man you have sex with dies, and you die with him. You belong to me now. Do you understand that or do I need to explain it?"

Real, total astonishment is not something you get to see all that often. It's when something you do not believe is real invades your world, and your mind struggles to make sense of it. That was the expression on her face.

"Are you kidding me?"

"Do you see me laughing? Why is it so funny? You said you had a crush on me. I like you. You're fucked up, but you're fucked up in a way I like. We can make serious money together and amass a lot of power. That's all good. But I don't want other men touching you. Your body belongs to me. And I don't want men laughing at me because you are screwing other guys. Even the bellboys in New York were laughing at you and Galkin because you were screwing one of your apes. That won't happen to me. I will be respected. You have a problem with that?"

She shook her head. She was expressionless. She was probably planning my death right there and then, but she said, "No."

"Good. How's your meeting with the minister of trade going down?"

"I have to drive to Colombo."

"How long is that going to take?"

She shrugged. "Ten hours. If I leave this evening, I'll be there tomorrow morning for breakfast."

I scowled. "And have one of your apes drive you?"

She sighed. "I have an arrangement with the minister, Harry. I can't have you drive me. What are you going to do, kill the minister for transport? If we want payment for those products, I need to honor our agreement."

"You need to call him to fix where and when you're going to meet, right?" She nodded. "So you do that from our room."

"*Our* room." She was smiling. I didn't return the smile.

"Yeah, our room. You have a problem with that?"

"None."

"Good. So you do that from our room. You leave me and the boys downstairs with CD. Any noise you hear, you ignore it."

"Jesus, Harry!" Her smile turned to a laugh. "You gonna whack him this afternoon?"

"Yeah. You better explain to your boys I'm taking over."

She shook her head, spearing a prawn with her fork. "I never told you you were taking over."

"So what? I just told you."

She watched me a while, chewing her prawn. "You be careful with me, Harry. I'm having fun right now. The minute this stops being fun, I'll kill you."

"Yeah?" I put a forkful of rice and spicy chicken in my mouth, chewed, and washed it down with beer. As I leaned forward for more, I told her, "You'd better pray *I* start having fun soon. I might just kill you when I'm done with CD."

It must have sounded convincing because she went pale with her fork halfway to her mouth, where it froze. I smiled. She smiled back, and we both laughed.

SEVENTEEN

THE HOUSE WAS A QUARTER OF A MILE'S WALK ALONG the beach around a small headland. It was enclosed behind a large, white wall set among a sprawling grove of palm trees. They hadn't exaggerated when they had described the house as a small palace. It was a sprawling, three-story colonial building with red gabled roofs and wraparound verandas. There was a pool and a tennis court and rambling walkways among flowerbeds under the palms. There were also a couple of Range Rovers parked out front.

We found CD sitting on the veranda by the door in a rocking chair. He watched us arrive without saying anything. As we climbed the steps, I told her, "Wait for me inside. You're going to show me our room."

She stepped through the double doors into a broad, spacious living room, and I turned to CD.

"Stick around. We need to talk. I'm going up with Larsen. I'll be down in a while."

"You giving orders now, Harry?"

"Looks that way, don't it?" I looked around. "Where are the boys?"

"Around."

"Gather them up. We're having a conference. Things are going to change around here."

His sigh was more of a groan. "Yes *sir*, whatever you say, *sir*."

I went inside and followed Anniken up a winding, white staircase to a galleried landing on the second floor. From there, I followed her down a passage to a door which she opened, and I followed her inside.

It wasn't a bedroom. It was a suite. We entered into a comfortable drawing room with a calico sofa and a couple of armchairs, heavy dark wood bookcases, and a coffee table. Behind her, there was a terrace overlooking the ocean. On the right, double doors stood open onto a bedroom with a huge, four-poster bed draped with fine, semi-transparent muslin. Beyond it was another terrace with its French windows open. I closed the door, and she turned to face me. She was silhouetted against the light of the terrace.

"Let's make this work, Harry."

In spite of myself, I felt my heart pound hard in my chest. I hated everything she stood for, and it was because of her and Galkin that Jane was in critical—or worse—condition. But when I looked at her, behind her almost angelic looks, I recognized a predator, a survivor, a creature who had no time for other people's rules, a creature who lived in the moment, for the moment, according to her own rules. I recognized a kindred soul, and every part of my mind rejected that fact, but my body was not listening to my mind. My body was otherwise engaged.

She said,

"Do you want to make it work, Harry?"

I didn't answer. She began to unbutton her blouse. She slipped it off over her slim arms and dropped it on the floor. "Come and show me," she said, "how you want to make it work."

At five p.m., she rose from the bed, pale and slender in the afternoon light, with the burnished, copper sun touching her breasts and her legs. I lay and watched her move to the en suite bathroom and move behind the frosted glass of the shower cubicle. Then there was the hiss of the shower, and the clouds of steam rose and enfolded her.

I swung my legs out of bed and sat staring out of the window at the Indian Ocean, where the great breakers cast spray high into the air before rolling, tumbling to the shore. After a moment, I reached for her cell phone, stood and moved to the French windows, and went out onto the terrace. There I punched in the Cobra code that would stop the call from being registered and called the brigadier. He answered immediately. He didn't sound happy. He sounded tense.

"Yes. Where are you? What is happening?"

I turned and leaned my back against the balustrade, looking in at Anniken's form as she lathered her body. "One of the problems with getting betrayed and kidnapped is that sometimes you end up killing the people who kidnap you. That can happen if the people who are supposed to keep you briefed and informed start playing stupid games and stop informing you."

"What are you talking about, Harry?"

"I'm talking about your friend, CD."

"He's gone AWOL. Is he with you?"

"He betrayed me. He and Anniken have brought me to Sri Lanka. There's a ship being held at the docks in Colombo with biochemical weapons for Russia and components for nuclear devices headed for Iran."

"What's the name of the ship?"

"She hasn't told me yet."

"CD...? I can hardly believe it."

"Yeah. I'm confused. He hasn't told her about Cobra or about you, and he's facilitating things for me to pose as a rogue CIA agent. You didn't instruct him to do that?"

"No."

I grunted. "Larsen has a meeting with the Sri Lankan minister for transport tomorrow in Colombo. She'll secure the ship's release, and from there, it will make its way to Konarak on the south coast of Iran. She won't make it to Colombo, but you'd better have your bases covered. We need the name of the ship."

"That won't be easy. Where are you now? Do you need extracting?"

"No, I've taken over Galkin's operation. I'm about to find out who CD is and what the hell he's doing."

"Be careful."

I hung up. Anniken had come out of the shower and was standing drying her hair. I slipped the phone in my back pocket and went inside. I walked over to where she stood in the bathroom and took her gently by the shoulders, turning her to face me. She smiled. I said, "Look at me."

She looked me in the eye, and I punched her on the tip of her chin. It takes very little force to knock someone unconscious if you hit them just right on the tip of the chin. I collected her in my arms as she fell and carried her to the bed. There I bound her ankles and her wrists, made a bundle of her socks, and stuffed them in her mouth, binding that tightly too.

For a moment, I stood and looked down at her, wondering whether it would be smart to finish the job there and then. But there was the issue of the container ship, Russia and Iran, and I had a feeling I might still need to use her.

So I got dressed, locked her in the room, and went down to the drawing room. I found CD sitting on the sofa, staring at a cold fireplace. He looked up as I approached. He didn't look like a happy man.

He said, "Where is she?"

"Where are the men?"

"Two at the back door playing cards. Two walking the grounds and two at the front gate."

"That's it? Six of them?"

"Yeah, I think you killed everybody else."

I sat in the calico armchair across from him. "I told you in Singapore the next time you pulled a stunt on me I was going to kill you. There are two things right now standing between you and your maker, CD. One is that the brigadier says he trusts you. Two is the fact that you've kept your mouth shut about Cobra. Now you had better come clean, pal. There is far too much at stake here for me to take chances. Who are you and what are you doing?"

"Three."

"What?"

"You said there were two things standing between me and my maker. There are three—the two that you mentioned and me. You're a tough, dangerous guy, Harry. But I happen to be one of those too." He pointed at me. "I am going to ask for a little bit more respect from you, *pal*, because I got to tell you, you are getting on my nerves. If it were not for me, *pal*, your ass would be feeding the fishes at the bottom of the Indian Ocean."

I held his eye a moment, then sighed and nodded. He had a point. "Okay, granted, but it might be a bit easier to do that if you stopped springing surprises on me. Now do us both a favor and tell me what the hell you're doing."

He shook his head. "I can't do that. But what I can tell you is I am not going to blow your cover. Also, we need to talk about Anniken. You haven't taken her out, right?"

"No."

"I figured you were going to wait. We need her to stop the shipment."

"You know the name of the ship?"

"I am trying hard to find out before you cut off my source. You want to tell me what your plan is?"

"So you can spring another surprise on me?"

He held my eye for a long moment. "Harry, I understand that you're mad at me, and I get why. I'd be mad too. But let me ask you something. Do you trust Buddy?"

"You know the answer to that."

"What did he tell you about me?" He gave me a moment, but

I didn't say anything. I didn't need to. He went on, "So believe me when I tell you, anything and everything I did I had to do."

I sighed. "Anniken won't be joining us. She's a little tied up right now." He nodded once, slowly. I went on, "Let's call the guys and explain the new arrangements to them." I gave him something that might one day have developed into a smile. "The idea is I eliminate you and take over."

"That's me, always playing Bob Hope to somebody else's Bing Crosby."

"Right. Why don't I believe that? You want to call the four guys from the back, and I'll go get the two boys at the front gate."

He smiled on one side of his face. "You giving instructions now, Harry?" He raised a hand to stop me answering, got up, and walked toward the back of the house, where sliding plate glass doors gave access to the pool and tennis court.

I left through the front door and made my way down the drive toward the front gate. I could see the two guys there looking bored and smoking. One of them looked Mediterranean, only he was big, maybe six-three, with a back the size of an aircraft carrier and a head the size of a small moon. He had black hair, olive skin, and a moustache you could create a nature reserve in.

His pal was smaller, maybe six foot, more athletic, with a military crew cut. I figured if the moustache was Turkish, this guy might be Russian. They were both watching me with eyes that were somewhere between indifferent and hostile. When I was eight or nine feet away, I said, "You speak English?"

"Yeah, English."

It was the Russian one. He looked more convinced than his bigger friend. I spoke slowly.

"We're having a meeting inside. You understand?"

He nodded. "Yuh, meeting."

"Anniken has decided she wants me to kill CD. Okay?"

Their eyes narrowed, and they exchanged a glance. The big one said, "You kill CD?"

"Not yet. I talked to Anniken. She said she wants me to kill CD. CD is inside. I want your help."

The smaller one spoke to the moustache in what sounded like Russian. The moustache answered in the same language, so I guess he wasn't Turkish after all. They both looked at me and smiled. I guess they didn't like CD. The smaller one said, "Yeah, okay."

I returned the smile and pulled the Fairbairn and Sykes from my boot. I held it toward him, hilt first, saying, "Just hold my knife for me, will you?"

He was still frowning like he didn't really understand when I flipped it and slipped the blade through the side of his neck. The moustache's eyes were huge and his mouth under the great black growth was a perfect O. That was as far as he got in his reactions because the kick to his balls was virtually simultaneous. My instep crashed home, and as he bent and wheezed, I delivered a right hook to his temple that would have ripped a smaller man's head off. He died and fell flat on his face with a big *whoof!* I guess that's how you make a grown man bark.

His smaller pal was on his knees. I removed the knife, and there was no great fountain of blood, so I guess he was already dead too. I wiped the blade on his jacket and made my way back to the house. As I reached the veranda, I pulled the Sig from my waistband behind my back.

Two of the guys were standing, the other two were sitting on the sofa. CD was in an armchair. They all watched me approach. When I was ten feet from them, I pointed the Sig at CD.

"Okay, pal, this is where it ends for you. Anniken wants you dead, and I am taking over."

He scowled. "What the hell!"

"You!" I jerked my chin at one of the two guys standing. "Go up to Anniken's room and ask her..."

That was as far as I needed to go. I had them all paying attention, listening to what I was saying. That would give me the four seconds I needed. I shot the two guys on the sofa while the two guys standing were still gaping at me. One slug each right between the eyes.

By the time I was done, CD was on his feet and had delivered two powerful hooks to his nearest guy's kidneys and I had popped a third slug through my man's brow. I figure he died wondering what it was he had to ask Anniken. CD broke his guy's neck, and we were done.

He looked at me as he dropped his guy to the floor and nodded. "Neat. The guys at the gate?"

"Gone to the great vecherinka in the sky."

He looked at the guys on the sofa and the floor. "Five," he said. "Buddy was right about you."

"Yeah? What did he say?"

"He said you were a very dangerous man."

I shrugged. "So we need to talk. I hear you and I agree, we need to stop the shipments, and we need to debrief her, but I need to execute my brief too."

He nodded. "That should not be impossible. Excuse me. I am unarmed and not comfortable that way."

He bent and took the Glock from the guy whose neck he'd broken. As he came up, he backhanded me with the butt of the gun, and for the second time, my world went dark.

EIGHTEEN

I don't know how long I was out. It couldn't have been more than ten or fifteen minutes, but I came around with a splitting pain in my head. I still had my Sig and my knife, but Anniken's phone had gone from my back pocket. I did the kind of cursing that gets you a special place in hell, staggered to my feet, and ran up the stairs. I might have saved myself the trouble. I knew they wouldn't be there, and as I stumbled up the steps, I saw through the windows that one of the Range Rovers was missing.

The bedroom was empty. Her still-damp socks were rolled up on the bed. I gave myself fifteen seconds to curse CD, his parents and his extended family, got it out of my system, and ran down the stairs forcing myself to ignore the pain in my head and in my ass, both compliments of CD.

I searched the corpses till I found a fob for a Range Rover. I took that and pulled his cell from his pocket too. I showed it his face and got inside, then configured it to my needs. Then I went outside, pressed the fob, and the lights flashed. I popped the hood and looked inside. I couldn't see any damage done, so I climbed behind the wheel and pressed the starter. It coughed. I tried again, and it coughed some more. That was when I noticed the fuel gauge. The tank was empty. I climbed out and saw the cap open, a plastic tube hanging out of the tank and a deep, large, very flammable pool of liquid on the tiles around the rear wheel.

Faster than and easier than pulling plugs, and once you've sucked on the tube, you can leave it to drain out all on its own.

The nearest gas station was a mile away across town. By the time I got back with enough gas to get me to the gas station, they'd be a hundred miles away and moving fast. I snatched the tube up and drained what little was left in it back into the tank. Then I sprinted to the house, to the kitchen and tore everything apart until I had a stainless steel pot, a plastic bucket, a kitchen towel, and a large sponge. Then I ran back to the truck, dropped on my knees, and started sponging up the gas, squeezing it into the bucket. When I had everything I could get, I laid the kitchen towel over the stainless steel pot and poured the gas over it to strain out the dirt. Then what little I had been able to recover I poured back into the tank. I figured, with just a little luck, it might get me the mile to the gas station.

I climbed in behind the wheel, pressed the ignition, and nothing happened. Nothing happened two more times and then the big engine roared into life. I eased out of the gate and onto a long, straight road that seemed to have no name. I kept the gears high and the speed steady, and after a couple of minutes, I came to the intersection with the Colombo-Batticaloa Highway. There I turned left onto a slight incline, put the truck in neutral, and let gravity carry me gently to the Lank Fuel Station. There I filled up and headed back onto the Colombo-Batticaloa Highway, this time headed west, at speed.

I checked my watch and was surprised to see it was already past seven p.m.

I had no hope of catching them. There were two of them and one of me. They could take turns resting and driving, besides which, CD was more than able to drive through the night without rest. The best I could hope for was to arrive within a few hours of them and track them to the ship.

Unless.

An idea wormed its way through the pain in my head. I pulled out the cell I had taken, punched in the Cobra code, and called the brigadier.

"Harry."

"The phone I called you on earlier, can you get the tech guys to trace that number and locate the GPS?"

He was silent for a moment. "I don't know. Probably."

"Three o'clock tomorrow morning, that phone will be in Colombo. Keep tabs on it, and it might lead you to the ship."

"I'll let you know as soon as we have it and patch it through to the phone you're on now."

"Good."

"Are you armed?"

"Yeah, CD left me my weapons."

"But you'll need money and clothes, I imagine. And a cell phone."

"Yes."

"What about extraction?"

"I haven't thought about it. Have we got a plane in the neighborhood?"

"I'll get you some papers and an air taxi through the embassy."

"Fine. I'll be in touch."

The hours passed as darkness closed in. Miles of dense rainforest separated one small, unpronounceable village from the next. Dombagahawela slipped by, a scattered procession of dark, silent huts; then Galabedda and high in the hills, Monargala, deep among the reaching trees, with its silent, empty twenty-four hour gas station.

The night rolled on, grindingly slow. The road climbed steadily, and steadily it deteriorated until it was little more than a mountain track, winding through tiny hamlets. And as I climbed, the blackness around me seemed to shrink the orange funnels of my headlights as I curled around one bend after another until, with sleep crowding in on me and putting sandbags on my eyelids, I began to dream I was driving into a twisting, glowing, amber tunnel.

I slammed on the brakes on the wrong side of the road, inches from the parapet of the bridge over the river Lamastota Oya, surrounded by steep hills and dense, black rainforest. I reversed to the beginning of the bridge and onto the roadside. There I climbed out.

It was cold and very quiet, but for the rattle and splash of the water falling down the mountainside under the bridge and the occasional cry of what I assumed was a bird in the trees.

I made my way to the bridge and scrambled down to the water's edge. It was slightly luminous in the dark, with the foam glowing where it was split and churned by the rocks. There I lay on the grass and plunged my head into the icy flow. It made me gasp and snapped me awake. So I stripped off my clothes, walked as far as a still pool, and plunged my whole body in.

That made me shout and roar under the water, but it woke me up fully. I scrambled out, pulled on my clothes, and ran back up the bank. There I climbed behind the wheel, fired up the engine, and roared across the bridge, shuddering and blasting hot air.

As I plunged first south and then west through the empty villages, I connected the gorilla's cell phone to the Range Rover's Bluetooth. The screen told me it was closing on one a.m. It wasn't late. I guessed the drugs, repeated blows to the head, and gashes in my back must be taking their toll. The GPS told me I was five hours from Colombo, which put my ETA at six a.m. It wasn't perfect, but it was good enough.

At three-thirty I slipped through the sleeping village of Tiriwanakatia, where all the buildings with their dark sleeping eyes looked like they were being engulfed and consumed by trees and creeping, overabundant undergrowth.

I was about to turn on the radio and find a heavy metal

channel to stop myself slipping into sleep again when my phone rang. I pressed the green icon on the screen.

"Harry, it's Buddy. How are you bearing up?"

"Just passing through Tiriwanakatia, wishing I could have a cold shower to wake myself up."

"It's a hell of a drive. I've had you booked into the Grand Oriental Hotel on York St, in the port area. They believe you have been mugged and are a friend of the American ambassador. They'll take care of you."

"Great. What about Larsen?"

"The GPS on her phone places her at a house at 103d Rosemead Place. They have just arrived there. I'm having the nerds look into it. So far, it seems to be a private residence belonging to the International Holdings Corporation, which will no doubt turn out to belong to the late Nick Galkin, or at least one of his companies."

"No doubt."

"So as far as we know, she is there alone with CD, but we don't know that for sure. So we need to proceed with extreme caution. I have asked the ambassador to keep a discreet eye on the place for the next day or so."

"The ambassador?"

"The British ambassador. He's sent a couple of chaps from the SIS."

"Can we trust them?"

"Yes, Gerald and I were at school together. He's an excellent fellow, and MI6 are our guys, Harry. Don't get paranoid on me. We are all on the same side."

"Yes, sir."

There was a noise in the background, like a door opening. I heard the brigadier say, "Excuse me a moment, Harry," then, "Yes?" There were voices, quiet, murmuring. Then the door closed again.

"Harry."

"What was that?"

I could feel my belly burning, and I didn't know why. He sighed. "Harry, you should focus on the task in hand."

"What was it?"

"Jane. She's gone into cardiac arrest. They are trying to resuscitate her."

I didn't say anything. I couldn't say anything. I just stared at the black road ahead with the encroaching trees closing in on either side, winding and twisting, going ever deeper into blackness. I heard him say, "Harry? Are you going to be okay?"

"Yeah," I said at last. "I'll just focus on the task in hand."

I hung up. The task in hand was killing Anniken Larsen, and that was what I was going to focus on.

NINETEEN

I ARRIVED AT THE GRAND ORIENTAL AT HALF PAST FIVE a.m. To say the outside reeked of faded grandeur would be unfair to faded grandeur. It was faded, and you could tell that once it had had grandeur. Right then it looked like it was struggling to make a living in the face of all the ugliness the port development had brought with it, the disreputable clientele that the 52 Stallion Club next door no doubt brought with it, and the huge police barracks that had been built on the other side. It made you wonder who those disreputable clients were in the 52 Stallion Pub.

I dismissed the speculation, entered the colonnaded porch, and pushed through the doors into the reception. I had to admit the inside had retained its grandeur, and the feeling of slipping back into the 19th century was oddly soothing. As I approached the desk, the pretty girl behind it smiled and said, "You must be Mr. Harry Bauer."

My smile was rueful in response. "I look as though I've just been mugged, huh?"

She giggled. "But you carry it with elegance and charm." She handed me a key. "Your clothes arrived from the embassy, and we have taken the liberty of hanging them in your closet." Her smile turned compassionate. "Will you be having breakfast, Mr. Bauer?"

I glanced at my watch. "Yes, eight-thirty in my room. Lots of black coffee and eggs and bacon."

She held out her hand. "Would you like us to park your car?"

I handed her the fob. "When I leave, can I take you with me?"

"Let me ask my husband. He'll probably say yes."

"Fool," I muttered and made my way to the elevators.

I had time to glance in the closet and see that the brigadier had provided me with three suits, a toilet bag, and a steel box which I knew would open with my Cobra code. Then I fell on the bed and sank immediately into a deep sleep. I was awoken at eight-thirty by the telephone and a sweet voice I recognized telling me a boy was at the door with my breakfast.

I groped to the door, let the kid in, gave him twenty bucks, shooed him out, and fell into the shower. Fifteen minutes later, I emerged human enough to eat breakfast, get dressed, and have a look in the steel box. It contained, as I had expected, a specially adapted Cobra cell phone, a box of ammo, ten thousand dollars cash, forty thousand Sri Lankan rupees, and a wallet with a credit card, passport, and an open booking for an air taxi to Malaga.

I took half the rupees and a couple of grand in dollars and made my out to the street. My instinct was to get the Range Rover, drive to her house, ring the doorbell, and shoot her where she stood. My brain told my gut that wasn't a great idea. This whole thing was about that damned ship, so the first thing I needed to do was to find the ship.

So I took a stroll down the Layden Bastian Road. There was a lot of construction work going on on what looked like a freeway, and where there had been some kind of perimeter wall to the docks with barbed wire and guard towers, this had been pulled down, and there was free access to much of the dock area via the Colombo Port Main Road. It wasn't exactly the kind of place where you'd choose to go for a stroll, but it looked like it was getting a major face lift, and there were shopping areas going up and even a couple of cafés.

I stuck my hands in my pockets and took a stroll past the Melbourne Jetty, the Prince of Wales Jetty, and the King's Jetty, looking like I had a real fascination with cargo ships. There were a lot of them, and there was no way of telling which one, if any, was Anniken's. My gut started telling my brain the smart thing would have been to grab Anniken by the scruff of the neck and make her tell me before blowing her head off.

After the King's Jetty, I strolled toward the Colombo Harbor, where the passenger terminal was. I didn't think the ship would be in that area, but beyond it was a container depot and a vantage point that would give me a wider view of the port. I was figuring if the ship had been detained, there might be an area where they put detained ships to keep them out of the way of other shipping. It was a long shot, but it was all I had unless diplomatic channels could get Colombo to talk. And the way things stood, that didn't look likely.

The road led me to a large traffic circle with a statue dedicated to a guy called De Azevedo. It was surrounded by wasteland that would probably someday be parkland, and three hundred yards beyond that was a harbor where I could see no ships. A couple of minutes more brought me to the harbor's edge. Thirty feet of large rocks separated me from the water, and a steel fence separated me from the harbor itself, where a couple of armed guards were watching me.

There was only one ship in there. It was a container ship, moored maybe three or four hundred yards away, but the name was clear and easy to read. It was called the *Norse Lady*. I smiled to myself. It wasn't a happy smile. Just for a moment, I felt sorry for Nick Galkin. For all his ruthlessness, he was just a schmuck like the rest of us.

I turned and made my way back toward my hotel. As I walked, I pulled the cell from my pocket and called the brigadier.

"Where are you?"

"At the port in Colombo. There is a large, empty harbor to the west of the port, and there is a solitary ship there with armed guards on the wharf. The ship is called the *Norse Lady*. Two gets you a hundred it's Anniken Larsen's ship and the minister for transport has sequestered it and wants his ransom."

"Good work. I'll make discrete inquiries, but I can't take action until you have executed Larsen."

"I'm on it. What about the colonel?"

"They managed to resuscitate her. But, Harry, it doesn't look good. She is very weak."

"Right."

I took a stroll back to the hotel and told the guy on reception I wanted to rent a car. He must have known I had a perfectly functional Range Rover in the parking lot because he looked at me like I was crazy but had every right to be. While he sorted it out, I went and had an early hamburger and a beer in the bar.

An hour later, I collected my anonymous, nondescript Toyota Axio and headed out along the A2, which runs south along the west coast. After a couple of miles, at the Kollupitiya intersection, I turned left and east onto the Liberty Roundabout. There I took the second exit up the Green Path, past the Viharamahadevi Park and the strange, large, elegant houses that stood among beautiful gardens behind shabby, dilapidated walls on that long, shabby, dilapidated street. Everywhere there were trees, abundant and green, and everywhere there was shabby dilapidation.

Green Path became Horton Place, and one block on, I turned into Wijerama Mawatha, took my second turning on the right into Rosemead Place, and pulled up outside her place. The house was enclosed behind a large, white wall. There was a heavy roller blind which I figured led to a garage, and next to it was an archway with a door made of iron bars, like a jail. Set into the wall was a keypad with a small screen, and just inside the arch was a small camera.

I hunkered down, spat on my thumb and rubbed it in the dust and the dirt, then I reached in and smeared the lens of the camera with the dirt. When I was satisfied with the result, I pressed the call button.

It started bleeping and kept that up for about thirty seconds. I had assumed Anniken would be out but CD would be in, and he would answer the intercom. I was going to tell him in my best Sri Lankan accent that I had a message from the minister for Anniken Larsen. But now it looked like nobody was home. I eyed the gate and wondered if I could slip over the top. I didn't think so, and a glance down the road told me the three or four people on foot and on bicycles were three or four too many.

Fifteen or twenty feet from the gate, there was an alleyway. I rang again on the intercom, and while it bleeped, I took a stroll to the corner to look down the alley. Like everything else in Sri Lanka, it was rich with abundant vegetation, which in turn provided shadows and cover. I ambled down and found the wall there was about seven feet high, topped with an iron railing. I heard the bleeping of the intercom stop. I gave a small jump and took a firm hold of the iron railing. I pulled myself up, slipped over the railing, and let myself fall into a narrow path bordered by flowerbeds that led from the front of the house to the lawn at the back.

I headed for the lawn.

The lawn was a good thirty feet square with a swimming pool at the far end, a couple of recliners, a table with an umbrella, and some chairs. There was a path that skirted the grass and was itself flanked by rose beds. Beyond the rose beds, there were trees I could not identify, though at regular intervals among them were tall, slender palms.

There were two doors in the back of the house. One was on a terrace at the top of five broad terracotta tiled steps. This had a large plate glass sliding door. The other was farther over, at the tope of five more modest steps, and had the look of a kitchen door.

I walked to the pool and had a look. The tiles were wet around the table, but there was no trail of wet footsteps anywhere.

It was a warm day, but it was humid; the water might have been splashed there anything up to an hour earlier or more.

I crossed the lawn and climbed the steps to the sliding patio doors. The hairs on the back of my neck prickled. Whoever had come in from the pool had left the sliding doors open half an inch. Was it a trap? Or arrogant carelessness?

My gut told me it was the latter. If CD had left me alive, I was pretty sure he had not told Anniken. She expected me to be dead, and CD had probably been promoted to chief male again.

I slid the door open. I was in a small room with a very large TV. There were a couple of sage green armchairs, a matching sofa, a small fireplace, and English hunting prints on the walls. The carpet was thick and also sage green with a beige pattern. There were a couple of damp footprints just inside the door. One was large, the other was small. I pulled my Sig from under my arm. I hunkered down and waited, listening to the house. It was silent.

I crossed the room to the door and opened it onto a short passage. On my left, there was a wall, and on the right, about twelve feet away, three broad steps rose into a much bigger, broader room with a large dining table, a raised, copper fireplace in the center, and a seating area. The far wall was all glass and showed an abundant tropical garden. There was nobody there.

As I crossed the room, I saw behind me a broad staircase climbing to the upper floor. I paused again and listened. I wondered for a moment if CD had gone with her to meet the minister. But I figured if they had any hope of getting that container in her name again and on its way to Konarak in Iran, she would have to go alone. So maybe he'd driven her and was going to wait for her, like her pimp. The bitterness of the thought surprised me, and even as it crossed my mind, I dismissed it. The minister would want his pound of flesh. He'd want to wine her and dine her and then spend the night with her. There would be no point in CD waiting.

I went to the stairs and climbed them to the upper floor. There was a corridor. It was straight, and at the end, there was a window with a gable arch that afforded a view of more trees. On the left, about halfway down, there was a narrow door. My instinct told me it was where the maid kept the brooms and the vacuum cleaner. Another, bigger door suggested a bedroom. On the right, there were two doors, and both of those said bedroom too.

I opened the first one and looked in. There was a mattress wrapped in plastic on the bed and a couple of chairs draped in sheets. I checked the closets and an en suite bathroom but found nothing of interest.

The second room was bigger. It had a rumpled double bed, and there were clothes, male and female, on the floor and draped on various pieces of furniture. There was nobody in the walk-in closet or in the en suite bathroom.

I crossed the corridor to the third door and went in with the Sig held out straight ahead of me. It was an office. There was a large, oak desk ahead of me across the room. There was a desktop computer on it and various files. On my right, there was a dark, Castilian credenza with a silver tray of decanters and crystal glasses. On my left was a worn chesterfield with two chairs, and to the left of the desk French windows standing open, leading to a terrace. On the terrace I could just make out some cane chairs and a table.

I went and stood in the doorway. CD was sitting there, looking out at the abundant trees and the palms. He had a pot of coffee beside him and a half empty demitasse. And this one was definitely half empty and not half full.

He didn't have a lot of hair, so it wasn't hard to find the puncture wound. It was at the base of the skull, just above the first vertebra. In the old days, she would have used a hatpin, but not Anniken. Anniken had probably used a good old-fashioned ice pick.

I went to the balustrade and stood looking down at the pool. When I turned back to face CD, he looked sad. He looked like he'd died knowing what was happening to him, but the poor bastard had given up the fight. That's the power of women like Anniken. It's not that you can't fight them—physically they are weak and frail—it's that they are vampires, and they rob you of the will to fight them. They suck you dry, and you're grateful when they kill you.

TWENTY

My cell buzzed. I pulled it from my pocket. It was the only person it could be: the brigadier. But he had no reason to be calling me. I felt a hot pit in my belly. I thumbed green.

"Yeah?"

"Where are you?"

"At the house. CD is dead."

"You killed him?"

"No. He was sitting on the terrace, and somebody put an ice pick in the back of his neck."

"Poor bastard. We're tracking her GPS. She is leaving Colombo with the minister. That's not what we expected. We thought they'd dine at a restaurant and go to a hotel or a private apartment."

"That's what I had assumed." I spoke half to myself. "I expected her to do her deal with the minister, she'd come back here with her bill of lading, and the ship would take off for Iran..."

"But...?"

"But with CD dead, she had no intention of coming back here." And suddenly it was clear to me, and I swore violently. "Where is she headed?"

"North along the Hendala Hunupitiya Road. They're about

five miles out of town now and show no signs of stopping or returning."

"Your MI6 guys with them?"

"Keeping a discreet distance, yes. The minister has a chauffeur and a bodyguard with him."

"Tell them I am going after Anniken. Patch me through the GPS tracker. I need to know exactly where they go. They have to be stopped."

"What are you thinking?"

"The biochemical weapons, the plutonium, it's not on the damned ship anymore. The minister has had it transferred. Sir, they are headed for an airfield!"

"Sweet Jesus!"

"And sir, there is no way you are going to convince the Sri Lankan Air Force to shoot down one of their own government ministers. It is just not going to happen."

"Go."

I ran. I took the stairs six at a time and skidded across the living room headed for the front door. Before I got there, I saw what I realized was the entrance to the carport. I wrenched it open and saw what I had hoped to see. Neither Galkin nor Anniken would be seen dead in a Toyota Axio. They would drive a Bentley Continental Mulliner W12, six hundred and fifty horses, two hundred and eight miles per hour and zero to sixty in three and a half seconds.

I wrenched open the door and climbed behind the wheel. Thirty seconds' search found me the fob and the remote for the garage door under the armrest, and I was pulling out onto Rosemead Place. Two minutes after that, I was roaring down the AC5 toward Peliagoda and the coast. On the way, the brigadier's nerds patched me through to the GPS tracking, and I connected my cell to the Bentley's Bluetooth so I could follow them on the screen.

At Modara, I turned north onto the Negombo Road and floored the pedal. I roared over the Mattakkulia Bridge and was out of the city and into the suburbs. On the screen, I could see the blip that was Anniken and the minister. They were moving steadily north along the same road I was on, and I was closing on them slowly. My mind was racing as fast as the massive engine I was driving, trying to work out what the hell I was going to do when I caught up with them. I didn't rate the minister as dangerous, but the chances were his chauffeur and bodyguard were seasoned pros. Anniken was about as dangerous as they came. But even supposing I neutralized the four of them, I had no idea where they were headed, what their plan was or whether they had more men waiting. And with no intelligence, making a plan was just about impossible.

Then, just past Uswetakeiyawa Beach, the blip slowed and turned right onto Church Road. This road they followed at a sedate pace, winding through countryside and passing what looked like small villages. And at about the time I reached the intersection with Church Road, kicking up dust and making the tires squeal, they were turning right again at St. Nicholas Church, Bopitaiya.

The road they were on had no name. It was more of a neat dirt track between cottages, but it led east, out of the village of Bopitaiya and into the more remote countryside. And by the time I had reached St. Nicholas Church and turned right onto the nameless street, Anniken and the minister had slowed to a crawl among fields.

Then they stopped. They were about a mile away as the crow flies, a mile and a half, or maybe two, following the winding path through the fields. I sighed, seeing, bit by bit, how curious people came out of their houses and into their yards and gardens to look at the Bentley where it sat, silent and menacing outside their church. It had gotten me where I wanted to go, and fast, but now it was about as anonymous as a strippergram at a vicar's tea party.

I put the beast in drive and rolled quietly down the road. Pretty soon, I had left the village and the quaint houses behind and was moving among fields and areas of dense undergrowth. Here and there, a path led off the track and in among trees and ferns. When the screen told me I was three hundred yards from Anniken's phone, I pulled off the road and nudged the car in among the dense foliage. There I killed the engine and sat and thought. Ideally I would use the cover of darkness to get close and work out a plan of action. But the worst case scenario was that they would climb out of whatever vehicle they had arrived in and board their plane immediately.

A plane I didn't even know existed.

I had to play the only card I had and play it now. And to hell with the consequences.

I climbed out of the car, scrambled through a wall of dense trees, and found myself at the edge of a large, marshy field with a pond at the far end. About fifty yards to my right, there was a ditch with a hedgerow running along it, and if I followed that, I figured I could reach the far end of the field, about two hundred yards away, unseen. There, there was another wall of trees, and if my calculations were right, Anniken and her minister were on the other side of those trees.

A steady, crouching run with a few dives for cover got me across the field in something less than five minutes. There I dropped and crawled through the damp earth and dense foliage until I came to another ditch on the far side. There I inched up to the edge and peered over.

There was a driveway that curled around a pond to a large, Edwardian manor house fronted by extensive lawns. There was an SUV parked outside the front of the house, and there I could see Anniken with a heavyset man in a suit. He had very black hair and olive skin and two got me twenty he was the minister. They were talking to two guys in military fatigues with assault rifles.

Beyond the house and slightly to the right, maybe four hundred yards from where I was lying, I could see an old twin turboprop Hawker Siddeley 748. It was a medium haul cargo plane that could make it to the south coast of Iran with no problems. At a cruise speed of just short of three hundred miles an hour, it could cover the distance in less than six hours—a damned sight faster that the *Norse Lady*.

I thought about it for a minute. If I could get a bit closer, I could probably take all four of them with the Sig. I had the advantage of surprise. First the minister, then the two grunts in almost simultaneous shots. Then Anniken. It could probably be done, but it left the problem of the plane and its cargo.

Plus I didn't know what kind of army he had inside the house. There might be nobody, or he might have a small battalion in there. I closed my eyes and silenced my brain. What came to me was that I had no time to think. I had to act.

As I made that decision, Anniken and the guy turned away and headed for the broad steps to the front door, and the two guards took up positions at the foot of the steps. A moment later, two more men in uniform came out of the house. One turned left, the other turned right, and they began a slow patrol of the perimeter.

I made myself comfortable and gave myself ten minutes to time their circuits of the house. I worked out it took them four minutes to walk around the house, and they were well trained because they always crossed at exactly the same point at the front and the back. So their least vulnerable points were at the front and back of the house, and their most vulnerable points were while they were walking away from each other at the rear corners.

With that knowledge established in my mind, I took my time crawling along the ditch and around the expanse of lawn at the front of the house. I kept close among the trees in the hedgerow and moved slowly with no sudden movements. And pretty soon I saw what I had hoped to see: two soldiers guarding the plane. They had the hatch open behind the cockpit and the steps down. One of them was sitting on the steps. The other was standing, and they were smoking and talking quietly.

I continued around till I was at the far side of the plane. There I lay in the undergrowth and tried to piece together what little information I had into a basic plan of action.

It was clear that the minister was getting more out of this arrangement than simply satisfying his carnal appetites with the Nordic Nymph, but equally it was clear that satisfying his carnal appetites was part of the deal. A Hawker Siddeley 748 adapted for cargo transport was not a transport minister's idea of a romantic soirée, especially if the alternative is an Edwardian manor house, and you are fairly sure your two main enemies are dead.

This meant I had at least a little time before the plane took off.

My ideal time for action would be as dusk fell and visibility began to diminish. At that time, and with extreme speed, I needed to kill the two guys guarding the plane, preferably without being noticed. Then take out the four guys guarding the house, kill the minister for transport, grab Anniken, drag her to the plane, bind her hand, foot, and mouth, and fly the plane out into the middle of the Arabian sea. There I would either ditch it—if there were parachutes onboard—or try to land it on a US aircraft carrier.

Good plan. It was a good thing I'd come armed with a 9 mm semi-automatic and a knife.

I settled to rest and run over the thousand and one things that could go wrong with the plan and how I would respond in each case. Late afternoon began to move toward dusk after a couple of hours, and as the air turned grainy, I put all thoughts out of my mind and began to crawl very slowly on my belly toward the plane's landing gear. I made it to the nearest wheels and paused to draw the Fairbairn and Sykes from my boot.

I could hear their voices. They were talking softly, occasionally laughing. Slowly and by degrees, I moved around the wheel and diagonally toward the back of the steps. Here I paused again. I needed to psych myself. The action had to be very fast and flawless. I closed my eyes and visualized it several times.

Then I came around the steps and stood and smiled at them. There was astonishment on their faces, but these were trained men, and I knew I had two seconds, maximum three. The movement had to be slick and virtually simultaneous.

The guy sitting on the steps was maybe eighteen inches

away from me. The guy who was standing facing him was a stride away. With explosive savagery, I slammed the fighting knife into the sitting guy's neck. As the hilt rammed home, I was stepping toward his pal with my left foot and my right instep smashed up in an ark between his legs. That pain is so crippling all you can do is wheeze. While he was wheezing, I smashed a right hook into the side of his head, and he went gratefully into oblivion.

The guy on the steps had died swiftly and was sitting motionless. I grabbed his pal by his ankles and dragged him out of sight behind the landing gear. To be on the safe side, I broke his neck.

I returned to the steps and retrieved my knife. I hunkered down beside the steps and waited for the patrol to pass down beside the house. Then I crouch-ran to the nearest palm tree and dropped on my belly. I watched the guard come up from the front of the manor and walk along the side. He turned the corner, and I knew I had seventy-five seconds.

I sprinted silently across the lawn, hit the side of the house, and made for the back corner. There I flattened myself against the wall with the Fairbairn and Sykes clenched in my fist and waited, counting down the seconds.

He came around the corner on seventy-three, and I drove the blade up through his esophagus and out through the vertebrae in the back of his neck, severing his spinal cord. From that point on, whatever his brain thought his body should be doing, it couldn't get the message through. So his body twitched, his hands and his feet twitched, his eyes bulged, and he died.

I hooked him under his arms before he went down and dragged him back to the rear of the house and dumped him behind some rosebushes in the growing shadows. In my mind, I was counting down the next seventy-five seconds before his pal arrived from the front of the house.

With thirty seconds to spare, I flattened myself against the wall again. Only this time I was at the back of the house and the guard was approaching from the front. He would not expect to see his pal until he rounded the corner. By that time, it would be too late.

He came around bang on time, and with my left hand, I rammed the fighting knife through his throat, severing his spinal cord, bringing death in a couple of quivering seconds. I didn't bother hiding his body—there would be no one coming to find it—but I took his side arm and the Bushmaster M4 he'd had over his shoulder.

Logic dictated that these guys would have to be relieved, as would the two guys on the door, probably in about four hours if the plane had not departed by then. So somewhere in the house, there were probably at least four more soldiers, as well as Anniken and the minister.

And they would all have to die.

TWENTY-ONE

Dusk was turning to evening, the only light was from the lighted windows of the manor, and visibility was low. After a moment's thought, I pulled on the dead guy's uniform, slung his assault rifle over my shoulder and, without giving myself time to think about what I was doing, I trotted around the corner and ran at a jog along the front of the house toward the steps. It wasn't an urgent run, and I didn't express panic, so all it elicited from the guys on the door was a frown, and one of them moved toward me saying something in Sinhala or Tamil. I jugged up the three steps. It probably took one and a half seconds, and as we closed, I drove the knife into his throat. But the other guy was already on alert, and his Bushmaster was coming off his shoulder as his pal went down.

He was drawing breath to give the alarm as he tried to take aim. A 9 mm round through his forehead stopped both actions but gave the alert. I holstered the Sig and put my Bushmaster to my shoulder as I ran through the front door into the house.

There was a large entrance hall with a black and white checkerboard floor. An elegant marble staircase rose from the center of the room and curled to either side like rams' horns to meet a galleried landing. There were potted palms on either side at the foot of the stairs. There was no sign of people.

I ran past the stairs and down a short passage. A short flight of three steps and a cream door found me in a kitchen. There were two guys in uniforms wearing aprons. They were cooking, but they stopped to stare at me. The door slammed behind me, and I shot them before they ever knew I was a danger.

Thinking fast, I checked all the lower cupboards for either propane canisters or a gas main. I found two large canisters, and in a large pantry, I found two full replacement canisters. I pulled them out and stashed them by the stove. Then I found a wooden spoon, smothered it in oil, and set fire to it. I stuck that in a roll of kitchen paper, cut the hoses on the two propane canisters so they were both hissing hard, and ran from the kitchen back to the hall.

I was halfway up the elegant marble staircase when I heard two speeding Jeeps and at least one Land Rover screech to a halt outside. Then it was the tumble of running boots jumping from the vehicles and the bellowing of a sergeant's voice as he saw the dead men.

By the time they made it through the door, I was at the curve of the stairs on one knee behind the balustrade. I opened up with two triple taps, taking down the two first men through the door before the men behind returned fire. By that time I was running, counting in my mind how many I had seen and how many there might be.

I figured two Jeeps and a Land Rover made twelve to fourteen men.

He hadn't been expecting trouble, but she had. So he had six men at the house and a handful at a cottage on the grounds. Some arrangement like that. Either way, they had heard the shots and called for backup, and now I needed to find their suite before the soldiers got to them. This flashed through my mind in a millisecond as I heard more shouts and the boots tramping up the stairs at a run.

I got to the galleried landing and let off two bursts down the stairs, screaming in my mind at the gas canisters in the kitchen to quit fooling around and give me something. They gave me nothing, and I dropped to my belly, scrambling along trying to review in my mind where the nicest views would be. Because that's where the master bedroom was. It is not an easy thing to think about when you have more than a dozen men storming toward you with assault rifles.

I decided on back left, let off another couple of bursts, and ran, followed by a hail of hot lead. I skidded around a dogleg with the cold, dawning realization in my mind that I had come to the end. There was no way out of this, and I was about to die. It came with the strange, cold realization that the colonel, Jane, was at that moment dying too.

Those thoughts passed through my mind semiconsciously. At a conscious level, I saw the big, double doors that had to be the master bedroom. I ran like I had the hounds of hell on my heels, and as I ran, I opened up with the Bushmaster, blasting four rounds through the lock and the handle, ripping the wood to shreds. I hurled myself at the doors. They burst open, and I rolled across the floor on the other side. Somewhere in my mind, I was aware that the room I was in was immediately above the kitchen.

I rolled up on one knee with the assault rifle aimed at the open door. Then everything happened in slow motion. I saw I was at the foot of a huge, four-poster bed. There was a man in silk pajamas and a silk dressing gown—the same man I had seen downstairs with Anniken—his face a mixture of terror and rage. Kneeling on the bed in a black leather bikini and black leather boots was Anniken. In her hand she had a leather whip. In the doorway, six soldiers with assault rifles were colliding with each other. I roared as I opened fire on them and leapt in two strides across the foot of the bed toward the minister.

I saw the nearest soldier stop dead as three black-red holes erupted in his chest. Beside him, another threw his head back as his brains sprayed out the back of it. By that time, I had a fistful of the minister's hair and I was dragging him in front of me with the Bushmaster's cannon shoved against his right ear.

The doorway steadily filled with soldiers. I counted ten, with a sergeant at their head. He looked worried and a little mad. I ignored him and snarled at Anniken, "Lie face down on the bed or I'll blow your brains out." She was the only person in the room I figured was really dangerous. She stared at me but didn't do anything.

"CD said he'd killed you."

"He exaggerated. Understand this, my instructions are to take you out and disappear. CD asked me to get you to the CIA. You are pushing your luck. Lie face down or I will kill you and make my own life a lot easier."

She lay face down. I looked over at the sergeant. He said,

"Your position is hopeless. Hand over your weapon. You cannot get—"

I shot him between the eyes and scanned the faces of the nine remaining men. "Anybody else got an opinion on that?"

They aimed their rifles at me, but in so doing, they aimed them at the minister too. He screamed at them, "*Lower your weapons, you fools!*"

The explosion rocked the entire house. The glass in the windows erupted in glittering showers. Clouds of dust puffed out of the walls, the floor, and the ceiling. Even the air seemed to move in a muted slap. For a fraction of a second, nothing happened.

The gas from the two canisters had seeped through the kitchen and crept into pantries, slowly filling the kitchen, but it had taken its time because propane is heavier than air, so it had pooled around the floor until it had finally crept up the table and come to the burning spoon and the kitchen paper. Then it had exploded with such violence it had shaken the whole house, shattering windows and even damaging walls and ceilings. Above all, it had blown the regulator valves off the two other canisters. And for a second, as the kitchen caught fire, nothing happened. Then the two canisters, compressed and heated under extreme pressure, exploded.

In the bedroom, there was a violent smack, and the two canisters smashed through the floor before dropping back down. There was screaming, howling, and dust everywhere, and under my feet I could feel the floor creaking and slipping. Then the bed, which must have weighed half a ton, was slipping toward a groaning, gaping hole in the floor. It took me two seconds to empty my magazine into the panicking crowd of soldiers in the doorway before diving onto the bed and wrapping my arms and legs around Anniken as the floor gave way and we crashed into the burning kitchen in a shower of rubble, concrete, and plaster. The bed and the mattress broke our fall, but I kept my head covered as the debris showered around us.

Beneath me, I could hear Anniken screaming at me to get off her. I knelt with my knee in the small of her back and looked up through the dust. All I could see through the great, jagged hole, was the minister, white as a ghost with dust and plaster, his mouth sagging wide open and his eyes staring, with his hands to his ears. I took my Sig and put a bullet through the son of a bitch's head, then grabbed Anniken by her hair and dragged her screaming toward the kitchen door. She struggled like a wildcat, and I screamed at her through the ringing in my ears, "*You want to burn to death? You want me to leave you here?*"

The heat was intense, and the door was burning. I hurled her out into the passage, beating at my own smoldering clothes. She fell to the floor, and I dragged her up to her feet, thrusting my face into hers. "*Give me one, small excuse, Anniken! Just one small excuse! As things stand, maybe you get to live while the CIA picks your brains! Piss me off, just piss me off a little more, and you die here and now! Did I get through to you?*"

She nodded, and I dragged her stumbling through the house, out to the lawn and across to the plane. There I shoved her up the steps into the cargo area and smacked her in the jaw for the second time in only a few hours. I caught her as she fell, dumped her in the copilot's seat, and strapped her in.

Next thing, the turboprops were roaring, the whole damn plane was trembling, and we were away, hurtling down the dirt runway and lurching skyward. Then there was a kind of dark stillness behind the hum of the props. I pulled my cell from my jacket pocket and called the brigadier.

"Harry. Report."

"Can you fix my location from my cell?"

There was a moment's silence, then, "Yes. They're on it."

"The minister for transport is dead. So are eighteen of his men. I have the plane with the biochemicals in it and the nuclear material. I am in a blue and white Hawker Siddeley 748 headed toward the west coast of Sri Lanka, aiming for the middle of the Arabian Sea."

"Your plan being...?"

"Either ditch the crate and hope you find us or maybe land on a convenient aircraft carrier that happens to be in the area. I know we have at least one here."

"Bear with me..." He was gone almost a minute, then came back. "I am sending you the coordinates of the *Nimitz*. She is two hundred and twenty miles southeast of Al Hadd, in Oman. We'll contact the Indian authorities to give you a clear passage."

"Thank you, sir. I figure our ETA at about five hours from now."

"Harry, what about your target? As I understand it, the mission is not complete."

"No, sir. CD had asked me to bring her in to the CIA. I figured we needed whatever intelligence she might have."

He was silent for a long moment. Then he said, "Their network was virtually destroyed, Harry. With Galkin and her dead, there is nothing left."

"Right."

"Be safe, Harry. Keep me posted. No doubt I shall see you in a couple of days."

"Yes, sir."

I hung up and sat staring out at the blackness ahead of me, listening to the drone of the engines. After a moment, I turned to look at her. She was staring back at me with those big blue eyes. Suddenly her leather bikini and her black leather boots looked tragic. I was suddenly and painfully aware of how short her life had been, and how tragically wrong it had gone.

"Are you going to kill me?"

"That was my job."

"Let me go. Give me a parachute. I'll jump."

"How long do you think you'll last down there, in the Arabian sea?"

"Drop me over India. You'll never hear from me again. I'll disappear."

"How old are you?"

She frowned. "Twenty-four, why?"

"How many women, children, and old vulnerable people have died because of you in those short years? How many would have died if you had made it to Konarak?"

She narrowed her eyes at me. "Fuck you, you pussy!"

I switched the plane onto automatic pilot, pulled the Sig, and leveled it at her. She went pale.

"Harry, it was an outburst. I am sorry. You are right, but I am sure with therapy I can learn, I can change. It's a sickness. I have these multiple—"

I stood and moved to the back of the cockpit, covering her.

"You choose. You jump or I shoot you."

She scrambled out of the seat, reaching under it for the parachute. She showed it to me, making a question with her face. I nodded once. I followed her out to the cargo bay as she pulled on the chute. I gestured at the door.

"Open it."

She did as I said, and suddenly the place was filled with howling, screaming, sucking air. She stood at the black void of the arch with her soft, platinum hair lashing at her face, and that face was twisted with hatred. "*I will find you!*" she screamed. "*And I will kill you!*"

It was all I needed. I pulled the trigger and the Sig exploded in my hands. She fell backward into the night, plunging down toward the blackness of the Arabian Sea. I grabbed the door, slammed it shut, and spun the wheel. Then I returned to the cockpit and sat, staring at the empty seat beside me.

It was over.

EPILOGUE

There were funerals. Associates of Galkin's, directors of some of his companies, a senator renowned as an apologist for Islamic atrocities. One after another, they came down, a heart attack here, a skiing accident there, a road accident commuting to the office...

But one funeral overshadowed all the others. It was the one I never went to. Instead I sat on her bed in a special wing of the Cobra Headquarters in Pleasantville and played Ludo with her. For some reason, the fact that we both cheated outrageously made us both laugh more than was really warranted.

She was pale, an unhealthy yellow color, and she had shadows under her eyes, but she was out of danger, and every day she seemed to be a little stronger. The laughter and the cheating seemed to help.

Other times, we played gin rummy or Scrabble, and after a week, sometimes she would ask me to read to her, and she would drift off to sleep.

After ten days, I sat on a chair beside her bed and told her,

"I have to go home. Doc says you'll be up and about pretty soon." She nodded. I said, "You have any plans?"

She stared at the window a moment, then shook her head.

"Not really, Harry. I think I'm going to take early retirement. I've done a lot of thinking. I think I have proved everything I wanted to prove." She shrugged. "Or failed definitively to prove it, and now I think I want to spend some time deciding what *I* want to do." She smiled at me. "Not what my dad wanted me to do, not what my mom wanted me to do, and not the opposite either. Just, simply, what is *my* north star? And where can I follow it?"

I nodded, feeling oddly excluded for no particular reason. "That sounds good."

"And you?"

I shrugged. "I don't know." We were quiet for a moment, gripped by a fear no man could ever hope to inspire in me. I smiled at her. "Fearlessness is better by far," I told her, "than a faint heart, for any man who would poke his nose out of doors."

"Or woman."

"Right, so with that in view, I was wondering if, when you are fully recovered, and"—I gestured at her face—"more the color human beings are supposed to be, whether maybe you'd like to come for a week or two's convalescence either to a cute village in New England where we could eat oysters and drink champagne, or if you'd rather, somewhere in the Caribbean."

She stared at me for a long time in silence. Eventually she said, "Harry, I need to recover a bit more before I answer that question. Is that okay?"

"Of course." I smiled, in spite of the big hole in my belly.

"I need to know that you aren't upset."

I held her hand. "All I want is for you to get better and start being a pain in the ass again."

""I want to tell you, Harry, nobody has impacted my life—and impacted *is* the right word—quite the way you have. So my answer will probably be yes, so long as you don't blow up the hotel while we're there or shoot all the guests."

We both laughed. Then she looked sad.

"But Harry, if in a couple of weeks, or a month, I say no, I want you to know that it's because I like you too much. Does that make sense?"

"Sure," I said, and added, to myself, "If you're a woman."

I gave her a kiss on the forehead and, as I closed the door, I thought I saw her smirk, but it might have been a trick of the light.

1 See *A Simple Kill*

Don't miss BLOOD FOR BLOOD. The riveting sequel in the Harry Bauer Thriller series.

Scan the QR code below to purchase BLOOD FOR BLOOD.

Or go to: righthouse.com/blood-for-blood

NOTE: flip to the very end to read an exclusive sneak peak...

ALSO BY BLAKE BANNER

Up to date books can be found at:
www.righthouse.com/blake-banner

ROGUE THRILLERS

Gates of Hell (Book 1)
Hell's Fury (Book 2)

ALEX MASON THRILLERS

Odin (Book 1)
Ice Cold Spy (Book 2)
Mason's Law (Book 3)
Assets and Liabilities (Book 4)
Russian Roulette (Book 5)
Executive Order (Book 6)
Dead Man Talking (Book 7)
All The King's Men (Book 8)
Flashpoint (Book 9)
Brotherhood of the Goat (Book 10)
Dead Hot (Book 11)
Blood on Megiddo (Book 12)
Son of Hell (Book 13)

HARRY BAUER THRILLER SERIES

Dead of Night (Book 1)
Dying Breath (Book 2)
The Einstaat Brief (Book 3)
Quantum Kill (Book 4)
Immortal Hate (Book 5)
The Silent Blade (Book 6)
LA: Wild Justice (Book 7)

Breath of Hell (Book 8)
Invisible Evil (Book 9)
The Shadow of Ukupacha (Book 10)
Sweet Razor Cut (Book 11)
Blood of the Innocent (Book 12)
Blood on Balthazar (Book 13)
Simple Kill (Book 14)
Riding The Devil (Book 15)
The Unavenged (Book 16)
The Devil's Vengeance (Book 17)
Bloody Retribution (Book 18)
Rogue Kill (Book 19)
Blood for Blood (Book 20)

DEAD COLD MYSTERY SERIES

An Ace and a Pair (Book 1)
Two Bare Arms (Book 2)
Garden of the Damned (Book 3)
Let Us Prey (Book 4)
The Sins of the Father (Book 5)
Strange and Sinister Path (Book 6)
The Heart to Kill (Book 7)
Unnatural Murder (Book 8)
Fire from Heaven (Book 9)
To Kill Upon A Kiss (Book 10)
Murder Most Scottish (Book 11)
The Butcher of Whitechapel (Book 12)
Little Dead Riding Hood (Book 13)
Trick or Treat (Book 14)
Blood Into Wine (Book 15)
Jack In The Box (Book 16)
The Fall Moon (Book 17)
Blood In Babylon (Book 18)
Death In Dexter (Book 19)
Mustang Sally (Book 20)

A Christmas Killing (Book 21)
Mommy's Little Killer (Book 22)
Bleed Out (Book 23)
Dead and Buried (Book 24)
In Hot Blood (Book 25)
Fallen Angels (Book 26)
Knife Edge (Book 27)
Along Came A Spider (Book 28)
Cold Blood (Book 29)
Curtain Call (Book 30)

THE OMEGA SERIES

Dawn of the Hunter (Book 1)
Double Edged Blade (Book 2)
The Storm (Book 3)
The Hand of War (Book 4)
A Harvest of Blood (Book 5)
To Rule in Hell (Book 6)
Kill: One (Book 7)
Powder Burn (Book 8)
Kill: Two (Book 9)
Unleashed (Book 10)
The Omicron Kill (Book 11)
9mm Justice (Book 12)
Kill: Four (Book 13)
Death In Freedom (Book 14)
Endgame (Book 15)

ABOUT US

Right House is an independent publisher created by authors for readers. We specialize in Action, Thriller, Mystery, and Crime novels.

If you enjoyed this novel, then there is a good chance you will like what else we have to offer! Please stay up to date by using any of the links below.

Join our mailing lists to stay up to date -->
righthouse.com/email
Visit our website --> righthouse.com
Contact us --> contact@righthouse.com

facebook.com/righthousebooks
x.com/righthousebooks
instagram.com/righthousebooks

Printed in Dunstable, United Kingdom

67713840R00109